Four Men, One Lady, Six Guns

Charley got to his feet then and moved in on them. Clint and Dodge followed, but they were only backing him up.

"All right, Barney, throw your hands in the air, partner," Charley Smith said, gun in hand. Barney gave his wife a murderous look, as if he suspected her of leading the law there on purpose.

"Take it easy, Barney," Charley said. "She didn't know nothin' about it. I just decided we should follow her."

"Charley," Barney said, "you wouldn't shoot me, would you?"

"I'm wearin' a badge, Barney," Charley Smith said. "It's my job to shoot you if you try to escape. And if I don't do it, one of these fellas will."

Barney looked past Charley at Dodge and Clint.

"Damn it, Charley, he deserved it—"

"Don't admit to anythin' we'll have to swear to in court, Barney," Dodge said, quickly. "Just come along quietly."

Clint moved in, relieved Barney of a rifle and a six-shooter, and then took the six-shooter Linda Riggs was wearing.

"What were you going to do with this, ma'am?"

THE Gunsmith

340

THE BISBEE MASSACRE

J. R. ROBERTS

JOVE BOOKS, NEW YORK

THE BERKLEY PUBLISHING GROUP
Published by the Penguin Group
Penguin Group (USA) Inc.
375 Hudson Street, New York, New York 10014, USA

Penguin Group (Canada), 90 Eglinton Avenue East, Suite 700, Toronto, Ontario M4P 2Y3, Canada
(a division of Pearson Penguin Canada Inc.)
Penguin Books Ltd., 80 Strand, London WC2R 0RL, England
Penguin Group Ireland, 25 St. Stephen's Green, Dublin 2, Ireland (a division of Penguin Books Ltd.)
Penguin Group (Australia), 250 Camberwell Road, Camberwell, Victoria 3124, Australia
(a division of Pearson Australia Group Pty. Ltd.)
Penguin Books India Pvt. Ltd., 11 Community Centre, Panchsheel Park, New Delhi—110 017, India
Penguin Group (NZ), 67 Apollo Drive, Rosedale, North Shore 0632, New Zealand
(a division of Pearson New Zealand Ltd.)
Penguin Books (South Africa) (Pty.) Ltd., 24 Sturdee Avenue, Rosebank, Johannesburg 2196,
South Africa

Penguin Books Ltd., Registered Offices: 80 Strand, London WC2R 0RL, England

This is a work of fiction. Names, characters, places, and incidents either are the product of the author's imagination or are used fictitiously, and any resemblance to actual persons, living or dead, business establishments, events, or locales is entirely coincidental.

THE BISBEE MASSACRE

A Jove Book / published by arrangement with the author

PRINTING HISTORY
Jove edition / April 2010

ISBN: 978-0-515-14779-7

JOVE®
Jove Books are published by The Berkley Publishing Group,
a division of Penguin Group (USA) Inc.,
375 Hudson Street, New York, New York 10014.
JOVE® is a registered trademark of Penguin Group (USA) Inc.
The "J" design is a trademark of Penguin Group (USA) Inc.

PRINTED IN THE UNITED STATES OF AMERICA

10 9 8 7 6 5 4 3 2 1

ONE

Constable Fred Dodge walked past the Bird Cage Theater, stepped up to the front doors, and checked them. It was 4:00 a.m. All the doors in Tombstone should have been locked, even the Bird Cage. He rattled the doors, and then moved on, continuing his rounds down Allen Street.

Five years ago he had been in Tombstone during the whole Earp/Clanton thing. Since that time the legend had grown. Every story he ever read about the showdown had it happening in the O.K. Corral, when actually all of the principals had been on the street.

Dodge knew the whole story, though, because when he first came to Tombstone in 1879 he met and befriended the Earps. In fact, he and Morgan favored each other, so much so that he was occasionally called "Morg" while

Morgan had occasionally been called "Fred." They were good friends, though, and found it funny.

Dodge had done much work in this area of Arizona. In 1883 he was in Bisbee—twenty-three miles south of Tombstone—during the whole "Bisbee Massacre" thing.

So, the O.K. Corral in 1881, the Massacre in 1883, and now a constable during a time when Tomstone had become pretty boring.

But no one knew that, all during those times, he was also working undercover as a detective for Wells Fargo. Well, that wasn't exactly true. One man knew that he was a Wells Fargo man, but that man was also a very good friend of his.

His name was Clint Adams.

Clint rode into Tombstone at noon. It was not the Tombstone he had known back in 1881, and again in 1883. He hadn't been back since then. He had heard that the wild days were gone, so when he'd found himself fairly close by he decided to take a slight detour and have a look.

As he rode down Allen Street he wondered if the badge wearers in town were the same as the last time he was there. Fred Dodge had been there when he last left. Dodge was a good friend of his—so good, in fact, that Clint had been the only man in Tombstone or nearby Bisbee who knew that Fred Dodge was working undercover for Wells Fargo.

Dodge was good with a gun—so good that some called him a gunman. He had also owned a saloon for a while in Bisbee. And he had worked as both a constable and a deputy sheriff. And while holding each of those jobs, he had been working for Wells Fargo.

Clint also new Jim Hume, who Dodge had learned from. Those two men were the best detectives he'd ever known working for Wells Fargo. They were probably almost as good as his good friend Talbot Roper, the Denver-based private detective, and his other friend, the famous Heck Thomas.

Dodge—and his bosses at Wells Fargo—felt it was necessary for him to remain undercover as long as possible. So it was possible that he might have moved on to pursue his real job. If he hadn't, though, if he was still around, Clint felt certain he'd find Dodge wearing some kind of badge. Being a deputy was good cover for his undercover job.

Clint went through the ritual of freshly arriving in a town. First stop was the livery, which was being tended by a man he didn't know. The man was impressed with his horse, Eclipse, and promised to take good care of him.

Next move was to take his rifle and saddlebags over to the Sagebrush Hotel, one of the lesser known of the Tombstone hotels. He didn't want to attract any attention until he was good and ready.

After checking in he left his gear in the room and walked down to the Crystal Palace Saloon for a cold beer. If it had been later in the day he might have gone to the Bird Cage, where Doc Holliday used to deal faro back in the day. Now Doc was dead, and the Earps had gone their separate ways. He wasn't even sure where Wyatt and Virgil were at the moment.

He decided to nurse the beer and, when he was done, take a walk over to the sheriff's office to see who was behind the badge these days. He would be surprised if he walked in and found Dodge himself sitting at the desk.

However, before he even finished his beer the bat-wings opened and a man wearing a badge walked in. He looked around, but since there wasn't much to see—the gaming tables were covered, the girls hadn't come down yet, and a few customers were scattered—his eyes fell immediately on Clint, and brightened with recognition.

"Clint Adams?" he said, aloud. "By God, is that you?"

At the sound of Clint's name the few men in the place—including the bartender—perked up.

So much for keeping a low profile, Clint thought.

TWO

The next to last time Clint had seen Robert Hatch he had been running Campbell & Hatch Billiard Parlor, where Morgan Earp had been shot and killed. Two years later Hatch had managed to get himself appointed a deputy sheriff, and then elected sheriff. Apparently, that situation had not changed.

He approached Clint with his hand extended. Hatch and Clint had never been good friends, but they'd been civil to each other back in '81 and '83. However, Hatch pumped Clint's hand as if they were old friends.

"Well, whataya know?" Hatch said. "What are ya doin' in Tombstone?"

"Just passin' through, Bob," Clint said. "Looks like you've been doing a better job than your predecessor."

"I think folks around here woulda voted for anybody to get rid of Sheriff Ward."

Ward, now there was a man Clint remembered, and

had never liked. The people of Cochise County had found out very quickly that they'd elected the wrong man.

Whatever kind of sheriff Bob Hatch was, he had to be better than Ward.

"Well, congratulations," Clint said. "Who are your deputies?"

"You know 'em," Hatch said. "Charley Smith and Fred Dodge."

"Dodge is still around?"

"He is," Hatch said. "He's not only a deputy, but a constable, as well. The man is a hard worker, Clint."

"I know it," Clint said. "Do you know where he is now?"

"Not exactly," Hatch said, "but he should be in here shortly. Why don't you let me buy you another beer while we wait?"

"Sure," Clint said. It would save him the trouble of trying to find Dodge, himself.

Over fresh beers they discussed what had happened to them each in the past three years, where the Earps were, mutual acquaintances like Doc Holliday and Bat Masterson. Hatch finally finished his beer and turned down a second.

"I need to do my rounds," the man said. "Tombstone ain't the home for hellers it used to be, but I still like to keep my eye out."

"Sounds like a good idea," Clint said. The two men shook hands.

"Gonna stay long?" Hatch asked.

"A day or two," Clint said, "now that I know Dodge is here. Like to catch up with him."

"Stick around here," Hatch said. "He'll show up."

"Okay, thanks."

Hatch started away, then stopped and said, "Oh, almost forgot why I came in here." He waved the bartender over. "You seen Riggs?"

"Old Bannock or Young Barney?" the bartender asked.

"I'm lookin' for Barney," Hatch said, with a shrug, "but either one would do."

"Ain't seen hide nor hair of either one," the barman said.

"Then why'd you ask me which one?"

The bartender shrugged.

"You didn't say which one."

Sheriff Hatch gave the barman a hard look, then looked at Clint and said, "See you later."

"All right."

The sheriff left and the barman smiled.

"Giving the sheriff a hard time?"

The bartender looked at Clint. The man behind the bar was in his early thirties.

"Just havin' a little fun. Besides, Barney Riggs is a friend of mine."

"What'd he do that the sheriff is looking for him?"

The bartender shrugged.

"Hell if I know. Barney lives outside of town with his wife and Pa, Old Bannock Riggs."

"You think much of Hatch as a lawman?"

"You his friend?" the man asked.

"Not really," Clint said.

"Hatch ain't much," the barman said, "but I only got to town a few months ago. I hear he's better than the old sheriff."

"Ward," Clint said. "He wasn't worth anything."

"Hey, did he call you Clint Adams?"

"That's right."

"The Gunsmith?" the man asked. "That Adams?"

"Right again."

"Hey . . ." the barman said, but nothing else.

"What's your name?" Clint asked.

"Bascomb," the man said. "Carver Bascomb."

"Really?"

"What's wrong with it?"

"Kind of fancy," Clint said.

The man shrugged.

"That's my name."

"Hey, it's a fine name," Clint said, "just a little . . ."

"Fancy?"

"Yes, fancy. Can I call you Carver?"

"Yeah, if I can call you Clint."

"Deal."

They shook hands.

"Another beer while you're waitin' for Dodge?" Carver asked.

"Sure, why not?"

Carver drew him another beer and set it in front of him.

"You friends with Dodge?" Carver asked.

"Yes," Clint said, unequivocally. "Why? What's your opinion of him?"

"Truthfully?"

"Carver, when I ask you a question I want the truth. Always."

"Dodge is okay," Carver said. "So is Charley Smith. It's just Hatch I don't like."

"That's fine," Clint said.

"And I'm not sayin' that because Dodge is comin' through the door," Carver said, with a smile.

THREE

Fred Dodge had not seen Sheriff Hatch since that morning, so he knew nothing about Clint Adams being in town. When he walked into the Crystal Palace and saw Clint standing at the bar it was a complete surprise.

It was almost two o'clock when Dodge walked in the door. There were a few more patrons in the place, but not so many that Dodge couldn't spot Clint at the bar as soon as he came in. Clint could see the look of surprise on his face, and knew that Dodge either hadn't seen Hatch, or Hatch simply hadn't told him.

"What the hell—" Dodge said. He rushed forward and grabbed Clint's hand, pumped it warmly. "What the hell are you doin' in Tombstone?"

"Came to see you," Clint said. "Heard you were probably in trouble again, thought I'd help you out."

"Yeah, right," Dodge said. "What's the real reason?"

"To buy you a beer?" Clint asked.

"That's as good a reason as any," Dodge said. "Beer, Carver."

"Comin' up, Deputy."

Dodge accepted the beer and then said to Clint, "Let's go sit down and catch up."

"Deal."

"Want me to freshen that for ya, Clint?" Carver asked.

"No, that's okay," Clint said, and followed Dodge to a back table.

As he'd done with Hatch, Clint traded recent histories with Dodge, only there was much more concern and warmth involved.

"Hear anything from Wyatt? Virgil?"

"I saw Virgil a while ago, working as a private detective in Colton, California. Don't know if he's still there."

"And Wyatt?"

Clint shrugged.

"I don't know where he is now."

Dodge stared into his beer mug.

"Eighty-one was bad," he said, "bad for the Earp family."

"I can't argue with that."

"Wyatt lost his mind there, for a while."

Clint nodded. It was true. Wyatt's vendetta ride went on for a long time, until he'd tracked down all of the cowboys who were involved with the Clantons. After that, all the air seemed to go out of him. Then Doc died, and that seemed to take even more of a toll on him. Holliday was Wyatt's best friend, pure and simple. He was a deadly killer, but he loved Wyatt, and Wyatt felt the same. It was a relationship Clint had never been able to understand. He had good friends—Wyatt being one of them, along with Bat Masterson, Luke Short, Talbot Roper. But they were all good men. Doc Holliday had the devil in him, right up till the day that he died.

"What about you?" Clint asked.

"What do you mean?" Dodge asked.

"I mean . . . your situation. Still the same as it was in eighty-three?"

"Oh yeah," Dodge said, "still the same. Eighty-three." Dodge shook his head. "Bisbee, right?"

Clint nodded.

"Bisbee was a nice town," Dodge said. "Still is, in fact."

"What about Hatch?" Clint asked. "How's he as a sheriff?"

"Bob's okay," Dodge said, "better than ol' J. L. Ward ever was."

"That's for sure," Clint said. "Fred, why didn't you run for office?"

"No, not me," Dodge said. "My real job might take me out of here at any time. Deputy was as involved as I wanted to get. I could walk away from that, but I'd hate to just walk away from the sheriff's job, leave the town in the lurch."

"What about being a constable?"

"That's even more of a sideline," Dodge said. "Ike Roberts is still a constable, he takes care of most of those duties."

"Do you get over to Bisbee much?"

"Once in a while," Dodge said. "All my jobs take me there."

"Another beer?" Clint asked.

"No," Dodge said, "I got rounds to make." He touched the deputy's star on his chest. "I am wearin' this, after all."

"You going to be in town for a while?"

"Probably a few days at least," Dodge said. "Gonna stick around?"

"At least long enough for us to have a steak together," Clint said.

"Where are you stayin'?"

"Sagebrush."

"That dump?"

Clint shrugged.

"I was meaning to keep a low profile."

"Okay," Dodge said, standing up. "You want to meet up later tonight?"

"Sure. Bird Cage?"

Dodge nodded.

"For a drink," Dodge said. "Then we'll go and get that steak."

"I'll walk out with you," Clint said. "Think I'll have a bath and a haircut while I'm waiting."

He stood up and the two friends walked outside. Dodge slapped Clint on the back.

"I'll see you tonight at the Bird Cage," he said. "It's really good to see you."

"Yeah," Clint said, "you, too, Fred."

Dodge walked one way, and Clint headed the other, in search of a bath.

*   *   *

Clint had his haircut, then went to the rear of the barber-shop for his hot bath. As he entered the room and closed the door, the steam rose from the boiled water in the tub. That was good. It would take steaming-hot water to wash all the trail crud from his body. It felt as if it was baked into his pores.

He undressed, pulled a chair over by the tub to hang his gun belt on, then tested the water with his hand first, and then his big toe. He lowered his leg into the water up to his calf, hissed at the intense heat and pulled it back. He closed his eyes, lowered his foot all the way, then stepped in with the other foot. Little by little he lowered himself into the tub until he was up to his neck in hot water.

He closed his eyes and enjoyed the way the heat crept into his muscles. He used the soap and a cloth to vigor-ously scrub himself clean, then sat back again to just let his body soak in the heat. He didn't know how much time he had before the water started to cool, and he wanted to enjoy it as long as possible.

His mind floated back three years, to the day he first rode into Bisbee . . .

FOUR

BISBEE, ARIZONA TERRITORY
1883

As many times as Clint had been to Tombstone—the last in 1881 for the Earp-Clanton feud—he had not ever been to nearby Bisbee. Twenty-four miles to the southeast, Bisbee was also a town that was thriving on mining. Bisbee was easily larger than Tombstone, and thriving.

Clint had been returning from Mexico and when he realized he was so close to Bisbee he decided to stop and have a look.

He rode into Bisbee at midday, and the streets were busy. People were crossing the street in front of wagons from the mines, folks going in and out of the stores, a line of men in front of the assay office, waiting to have their metals weighed. Clint knew that the hills around Bisbee were filled with gold, silver, and copper, and that one of the biggest mines around was the Copper Queen

Mine. He knew that the Copper Queen had been staked in 1877 by George Warren, but he didn't know who owned it now.

The horse, wagon, and foot traffic was heavy in the center of town. Clint decided to rein Eclipse in, dismount, and find himself a cold beer. He knew Fred Dodge owned a saloon in town, so he figured to find that one.

He left Eclipse with his reins looped around a hitching post. If the horse backed up and pulled hard enough, he'd be able to get loose. Clint liked to leave the horse in charge of his own destiny. The animal would never wander away for no reason, and if he pulled loose there'd be good cause.

Clint started walking, occasionally stopping short so he wouldn't be run into by someone rushing in or out of a store. He reached a small saloon just as a man staggered out from between the batwing doors.

"Excuse me," Clint said.

"Yeah?" The man stopping, blinked, stared at Clint blearily. He was no kid, probably in his forties, so Clint figured he'd know every saloon in town. "Whataya wan'?"

"I'm looking for a saloon owned by Fred Dodge," Clint said.

"Across the street," the man said, pointing. "Only he don't own it no more."

"He doesn't?"

"He left town after the election."

"Did he leave Arizona?"

"Naw, he lives in Tombstone now," the man said. "Fact is, he got hisself appointed a deputy sheriff by the new sheriff."

"And what's his name?"

"Ward," the man said, making a face. "Already can tell he ain't worth a damn."

"Okay," Clint said. "Thanks."

"I'm goin' over there now," the man said, "only I can't walk so straight and I might get run down in the street. Wanna help me out?"

"Sure."

Clint walked the man across the street, holding him by the elbow, steering him that way. It was warm for December, but there were puddles in the street from recent rain. Clint not only kept the man from being run down, but from falling down face-first in some puddles. When they reached the saloon the man said, "Obliged," and went in ahead of Clint. Clint looked up and saw the name "Lily's" above the door.

Clint walked in, found himself in a small but well-appointed saloon. They were running a few games, had two girls working the floor. He walked to the bar.

"Help ya?" the barman asked.

"Beer, cold."

"Comin' up."

When he handed Clint the beer Clint said, "I hear Fred Dodge sold out."

"Yep, right after last month's election."

"You the new owner?"

"Naw, I just work here. New owner's name is Lily Farmer."

"A woman owns the place?"

"Yep," the bartender said, "and some woman."

"Good-looking?"

"Oh, yeah."

"Interesting."

Clint turned and leaned against the bar, working on his beer. He watched the two pretty girls work the floor, running it very competently between them. The dealers working the tables seemed to be legit.

He finished his beer, turned to face the bar. The bartender was right there, good at his job.

"'Nother?" the man asked.

"Later," Clint said. "I've got to get myself a hotel room."

"Well, you come back later on," the man said. "Lily usually comes down around nine to see how we're doin'."

"I'll check back," Clint promised. "Thanks."

FIVE

Clint got Eclipse situated at the livery stable, and himself set at the Copper Queen Hotel, then went and found a place to get a good steak. He knew the Cochise County Sheriff's Office was in Tombstone, the county seat, so he didn't bother looking for a lawman to check in with. He passed a few restaurants, but waited until he came to one that was doing a brisk business before going inside.

When the steak came it was worth the wait, cooked to perfection and large enough to fill the plate. The vegetables and onions were draped over the steak, the beer was cold. He ate it at a leisurely pace, taking the time to study the people at the other tables. They were mostly townsfolk, and he heard snatches of conversation involving cattle and mining, and even some concerning politics. Only a few tables seemed to be taken up by families, or married couples.

After he finished with his excellent supper he left and walked back over to Lily's saloon. The bartender's comments about the owner had raised his curiosity and he wanted to see if the man had been exaggerating.

He found the place jumping, but was able to secure a place at the bar for himself. The two girls who had been working the floor earlier had been joined by a third, and they all seemed to be working well together.

"You came back," the bartender said.

"I told you I would. A cold beer."

"Comin' up," the man promised.

When the man put the beer down in front of him Clint asked, "Boss around?"

"Not yet, but she will be."

"Hope she makes it before I finish my beer."

"If she don't I'll give ya another one on the house," the bartender said. "Believe me, it'll be worth the wait."

"Well, you've got me curious," Clint admitted, "and I never turn down a free beer."

The bartender went to wait on somebody else, and then another customer, and then two more. Clint watched him and saw that he was very good at his job, easily handling the work of two men.

He turned to watch the floor and the games. There was one roulette wheel, one faro table, a few poker games going on. There were some other tables in the back of the house, but he couldn't see what the games were— probably blackjack.

The girls came to the bar to pick up their drinks, gave Clint a flirtatious look each, then went back to the floor with their tray of drinks.

And then he saw her.

This had to be Lily, the woman whose name was above the door. The woman whose name made the bartender's eyes brighten.

She was tall, with lots of black hair piled atop her neck so that her long, graceful neck was in view. The low-cut deep blue dress showed off impressive cleavage that was creamy and smooth. As she came closer—although he knew she was simply walking to the bar, and not to him—he could see that she was breathtakingly beautiful. She had blue eyes—made even bluer by her dress—a strong nose, full lips, and a strong jaw. He'd started guessing her age at twenty-eight, but as she got closer he revised his estimate until he stopped at about thirty-eight.

"Larry," she called to the bartender. The men at the bar parted to allow her access, but they also turned away from her, averting their eyes. Clint wondered what that was all about.

The bartender leaned over the bar and the two of them had a brief conversation. Then he backed up and she turned around. Her eyes caught Clint's and held them, as if she was waiting for him to turn away, like the others. When he didn't she squared her shoulders and stared directly at him. He still didn't turn away, but neither did he approach her, or try to speak to her. In the end she looked away, then walked away, back into the crowd, which parted and then closed back up behind her until she was hidden from sight.

"What was that all about?" he asked the bartender.

"Oh, she wanted to know how we were doin'—" the man started, but Clint cut him off.

"No, I mean, nobody looked at her, except for me, and then she seemed to be trying to stare me down."

"Oh, that," the man said, grinning. "Was I wrong about her?"

"No, you weren't wrong."

"Well, almost every man in this place has tried to speak to her, get near her, gain her interest—something," the man said.

"And?"

"She cut them down," he said. "Made it so none of them even want to look at her."

"Why not?"

"They're afraid of her," he said. "She's embarrassed most of them, and they don't want to be embarrassed again."

"Does she have any friends?" he asked.

"Not that I know of," Larry said.

"Are you her friend?"

"I work for the lady."

"What about the other girls who work here?"

"They're afraid of her, too. She's on the town council, though. Knows pretty much all of the other merchants and businesspeople in town."

"Is she friends with any of them?"

"Not that I know," the bartender said, with a shrug. "Could be. Like I said, I just work here. I don't know much about her personal life."

"So there's no man in her life?"

Larry shrugged.

"I ain't seen one, but that don't mean there ain't somebody."

"Let me have that free beer, will you?"

"Comin' up," Larry said.

Clint didn't catch another glimpse of Lily once the crowd closed in around her. He took his fresh beer and decided to stroll the room, take a closer look at the games before he decided if he wanted to gamble or not.

SIX

Clint had decided against playing poker with a house dealer, so he played a little roulette, just to while away the time. He had decided to check out of his hotel in the morning and go to see Fred Dodge in Tombstone. However, while he was seated at the roulette table—even over the din in the saloon—he and the others heard the shots from outside.

He had just about lost the chips he'd purchased when he felt a tap on his shoulder. He turned, found himself looking into the eyes of the bartender.

"Can I—" he started, but the man cut him off.

"Miss Farmer would like to see you in her office."

"Farmer?"

"Lily."

"Really?"

The bartender nodded.

Clint took the rest of his chips—about twenty dollars—

and put them on number eight. When the wheel stopped spinning the white ball came to a stop on number eight.

"Eight a winner," the dealer said.

Clint stared. That was over seven hundred dollars.

"I'll have your chips cashed in for you—sir," the bartender said.

"Fine. Lead the way."

The bartender led Clint through the crowded casino to a door in the back wall. He knocked, and then opened it.

"Mr. Adams, Boss."

Clint slipped through the doorway past the bartender, who closed the door from the outside.

"Mr. Adams," she said, "I'm Lily Farmer."

Up close to her in the office, her beauty knocked him off balance.

"Mr. Adams?"

"I'm sorry," he said, "but you should be used to having your beauty make men speechless."

She stared at him for a long moment, then smiled. It lit up her entire face, made her impossibly beautiful.

"I see I'll have to watch out for you," she said.

"Why's that?"

"You seem to be a man who knows just what to say."

"Not always."

"Yes," she said, studying him, "I have a feeling it's always."

They stood staring at each other and the tension in the air was palpable. He had a feeling they were going to end up naked on top of her desk, and then the door slammed open.

"Sorry, Boss," the bartender said. "Something's goin' on outside. Shots fired. A lot of them."

Clint looked at Lily. Now he had a feeling they were not going to get back to this point in their lives.

"Go," she said to both of them.

There was a rush to get out the door. The shooting was still going on by the time Clint got outside, and seemed to be coming from one end of town. Clint ran that way, as did a few other men. Clint quickly realized what had happened when they reached the place. The bank and several stores had been held up. There were injured and dead people in the street, including a pregnant woman.

"That's Bob Roberts's wife," somebody said.

"This here's Johnny Tappinier and D. T. Smith."

"Are they dead?" somebody asked.

"Yeah."

"I got Joe Nolley and Indian Joe over here, both dead," someone else said.

Clint leaned over the pregnant woman. She was dead, shot twice, once through the heart, and another shot in the belly. Her unborn baby was surely gone.

A few men came out of the bank and the stores, and said, "We got hurt people in here."

"Here, too."

One of the men was Larry, the bartender.

"Is there a doctor in town?" Clint asked him.

"No, in Tombstone," he said. "Doc Goodfellow."

"Somebody's got to go to Tombstone for the law and the doc," a voice called.

"I'll go," Clint said. "I've got a fast horse."

"I'll go, too," Larry said. "My horse is at the stable."

"Come on, then," Clint said. "We better get saddled up. You folks do what you can for these people."

"What about the dead ones?" somebody asked.

"Take 'em to the undertaker," Larry said. "Mr. Adams and me'll be back soon."

Clint and the bartender ran for the livery and saddled their horses.

"You've got a good animal, there," Clint said, looking at Larry's dun, "but he's not going to be able to keep up with mine."

"That don't matter," Larry said. "You just ride hell-bent for leather and I'll do the best I can."

They rode out of town and before long Eclipse had outdistanced the other man's horse, and they left the bartender in the dust.

It was dark by the time Clint reached Tombstone. All he knew for sure was that Fred Dodge was a lawman there, so he stopped the first man he came to on Allen Street.

"Is Fred Dodge in town?"

"Deputy Dodge? Sure is. Just saw him over on the corner of Fifth, with Frank Ryan."

"Obliged," Clint said, and rode on for Fifth Street.

When he got there he saw two men standing on the corner talking. One of them was, indeed, Fred Dodge.

"Hey, Fred!" Clint called.

As Clint dismounted, Fred Dodge turned and looked at him in surprise.

"Clint Adams? What're you doin' in Tombstone, boy?" he asked.

"Right now I'm looking for you, Deputy," Clint said. "I just rode here from Bisbee."

"Bisbee?" Dodge said. "What were you doin'—"

"That's not important now," Clint said. "There's been a hold up there. People are dead and injured."

"Who's dead?" the other man asked.

"This is Constable Frank Ryan, Clint," Dodge said.

"I heard some names," Clint said. "Tappinier, D. T. Smith . . . and a pregnant woman named Roberts."

"Bob Roberts's wife?" Dodge asked. "They're friends of mine. She's dead?"

"Yes," Clint said. "Also Indian Joe and a man named Nolley. Might be more by now. They were hurt when I left. We've got to get the doctor."

Dodge turned to Ryan.

"You get Doc Goodfellow. I'll get the priest, and I'll wake Charley Smith. We'll meet at the livery and head to Bisbee."

"Right," Ryan said.

"The priest?" Clint asked, as Ryan ran off.

"Maybe he can do somethin' for the folks Doc can't help," Dodge said. "Come on. We need to get Bob Hatch and Charley Smith."

"Are they law?" Clint asked.

"Yeah, deputies, like me."

"Fred, are you still—"

"We got time to catch up later, Clint," Dodge said. "Right now we got to move fast."

"Right," Clint said, and followed.

SEVEN

They met up with Frank Ryan and Doc Goodfellow at the livery. They now had the priest with them, as well as the deputies, Smith and Hatch, and some other men. In the meantime, the bartender, Larry, had also gotten there.

As they saddled up, Larry said, "My horse won't make it back."

The man who owned the livery said he'd loan him a fresh mount.

"What about you, mister?" he asked Clint.

"Don't worry," Clint said. "My horse will make it."

The doctor was older, so they hitched up his buggy for him and the priest to ride on.

They returned to Bisbee at a gallop, arrived there in the middle of the night. The town was still awake, however, waiting for them to arrive. The street was lit by the torches the townspeople were holding.

"Where are the injured?" Doc asked.

"We got 'em in the hotel lobby, Doc. Over here," a man said.

The doctor and the priest followed.

A man approached on foot, and Dodge said, "Clint, this is Bill Daniels. He bought the saloon from me, and is also a deputy sheriff."

"He bought the saloon?" Clint said. He was going to ask about Lily, but it wasn't the time or place.

"Where's Ward?" Daniels asked, asking after the sheriff.

"We couldn't locate him, but we're here," Dodge said. "Me, Smith, and Hatch. We got some other men with us, including this fella who's a friend of mine—Clint Adams."

"Adams?" Daniels asked. "The Gunsmith?"

"That's right," Dodge said.

"Well, happy to have you, Adams," Daniels said. "We're gonna need you. Near I can find out, there was a gang of about five men."

"Anybody know any of them?" Dodge asked.

"No."

"Let's ask around, boys," Dodge said to Smith and Hatch. "Might find somebody who knows somethin'."

"Okay, Fred," Hatch said.

"Let's go and look in on the injured," Dodge said to Clint. "Maybe one of them knows something."

Clint nodded and followed his friend.

They entered the lobby of the Copper Queen Hotel, which had been turned into a makeshift hospital. The doctor was tending to the wounds of the injured, with the assistance of a few women from town.

"I have to talk to as many as I can," Dodge said to Clint. "I may be able to combine what little each of them knows. Meanwhile, why don't you see to your horse, and get some rest. We'll take a posse out at first light. If you want to come along—"

"I do," Clint said, quickly.

"Good," Dodge said. "I was hoping."

"I'll see you at first light," Clint said.

Dodge went over to the doctor to discuss the injured, while Clint left to take Eclipse to the livery. After a few hours the big horse would be ready to go. After riding to and back from Tombstone, he wondered if he could say the same for himself.

At first light Clint was back in the lobby of the hotel. There were less injured lying on cots there. Obviously, some of them had been able to go home—or perhaps they had died.

The doctor was still there, looking haggard and tired. He had two of the townswomen still assisting him.

"Doc," Clint said, approaching him.

The doctor looked up at him, squinted, then seemed to recognize him.

"Mr. Adams, is it?"

'That's right. Have you seen Deputy Dodge around?"

"Just a little while ago. I think he went down the street to find some breakfast."

"Thanks." Clint started away, then turned back. "Did you lose anyone during the night, Doc?"

"One," he said, "but I was able to send a few people home."

"Any of these folks in danger of dying?"

"No," the man said, "I think we're through the worst of it."

"Okay. Thanks, Doc."

The man nodded and went back to work.

Clint left the hotel and went in search of the place Dodge was having breakfast. He found it right down the street, as the doc had said.

EIGHT

It was a small café with about eight tables. He found Dodge sitting in the back, one of only two tables that were taken. His friend looked up at him as he approached.

"Mornin', Clint," Dodge said.

"Fred."

"Sit down. Had breakfast?"

"No," Clint said. "I thought we were leaving at first light."

"I've been up all night, Clint. I needed some coffee, and somethin' to eat. Have somethin' and then we'll meet the boys at the livery."

A middle-aged waitress came over, and Clint ordered eggs, bacon, and biscuits. She poured him some coffee and then went to get his order.

"Did you get anything?" Clint asked.

"I'm afraid I did."

"What? Somebody saw them?"

"Heard them," Dodge said.

"Heard?"

"Yeah," Dodge said. "Bob Hatch found a young fella who was able to imitate the voice of one of the men. I recognized it."

"You're kidding."

"No, I'm not."

"Well, who do you think it is?"

"Fella named Jack Dowd. The problem is, this don't seem like Dowd. He's a mule skinner, drove a twenty-mule team for Jimmy Carr a while back and always seemed to be on the square."

"So why would he do this?"

"I don't know."

"Any idea who was with him?"

"No, but I was out around Rucker Canyon a few days ago on a job. On the way back I passed an old ranch house. There were some men there shoeing some horses. One of them, a big man, looked familiar to me but I couldn't place him. Now I think it was Jack Dowd."

"But you didn't recognize the other men?"

"I didn't get that good a look at them," Dodge said. "How could I figure they'd do this a few days later?"

"You couldn't, Fred. Don't blame yourself."

"I'm good at what I do, Clint," he said, "but I missed somethin' here."

"I don't think so, Fred," Clint said. "I just think you're being too hard on yourself."

The waitress came back with Clint's breakfast. The eggs were cooked perfectly, and the bacon was crisp.

"This is good," he said.

"I used to eat breakfast here a lot when I lived here."

"You owned the saloon, right?"

"That's right."

"Lily's?"

"It wasn't called Lily's when I owned it."

"You said yesterday you sold it to a man?"

Dodge nodded.

"Bill Daniels."

"I was told that woman, Lily, owned it."

Dodge shook his head, poured himself some more coffee.

"Bill owns it, but Lily runs it. Have you seen her?" Dodge asked.

"Yes, last night."

"She's somethin', huh?"

"Seems like the men in this town are afraid of her."

"That's because she's a man-eater, Clint," Dodge said. "If you're settin' your hat for her you better beware."

"I'll remember that," Clint said. "Right now we've got other things to worry about."

They finished their breakfast, paid the bill, and walked to the livery.

"What kind of posse do we have?" Clint asked.

"My usual," Dodge said. "Charley Smith and me, we usually ride together. I also got the best trailer in the country, Manuel. He's part Yaqui, part Indian, and part Mexican. And then there's Bob Hatch, Frank Ryan, Bill Daniels, Sy Bryant, and a few others."

"Where are we going to look?"

"Might as well head for Rucker Canyon and see what we can find," Dodge said. "After all, that's where I saw them workin' on their horses. That is, unless Manuel can pick up their trail right away."

When they got to the livery, the other members of the posse were all gathered in front.

"Be right with ya," Dodge yelled, "soon as we saddle our mounts."

The others milled around impatiently while Clint saddled Eclipse and walked him out. Dodge came out last.

"Okay," he shouted, "we heard they rode out headin' north, so let's see if Manuel can pick up their trail. Let's ride out!"

NINE

Manuel did, indeed, pick up the robbers' trail outside of town. They followed the trail north, toward Bisbee Canyon. As they rode along, Dodge sidled up alongside of Clint.

"See that fella up front? With the blue shirt?" he asked.

"I see him."

"His name's John Heath," Dodge said. "A few weeks ago he came to town with a woman who is supposed to be his wife, opened up a saloon and dance hall."

"What about him?"

"I don't like 'im."

"Why not?"

"He just don't feel right," Dodge said. "Never has. I don't think he came to town to open a business."

"You think he came to town to case it?" Clint asked. "For the gang?"

"I don't know," Dodge said, "but I asked Sy Bryant to

keep an eye on him. He volunteered for the posse, and he don't strike me as the volunteer type."

"You think he's coming along to point us in the wrong direction?"

"Maybe."

"I'll watch him, too," Clint said.

"Thanks."

Dodge rode up to the head of the posse to ride alongside Manuel, who was still looking for signs. Clint put his eyes on Heath and watched him closely.

They got to Bisbee Canyon, rode in and then rode out to the north. There they all stopped while Manuel checked out the area. He dismounted and walked the ground, staring down intently, then walked to Dodge and spoke to him.

"Looks like somethin's wrong," Bill Daniels said to Clint.

"I think I know what it is," Clint said.

"What?"

"Look at the ground," Clint said. "I'm not a great tracker, but it's full of cattle tracks. Looks like the robbers rode in among the cattle to cover their trail."

Daniels looked down and said, "By God, you're right. Now what?"

"Manuel is supposed to be the best," Clint said, "and Dodge is no slouch. Somebody'll find the trail."

"Maybe you," Daniels said.

"Maybe," Clint said, although he didn't sound so sure.

It was getting late and they decided to camp there. With over a dozen men in the posse they made two fires and got two frying pans and coffeepots going for their meal. John Heath was sitting at the fire with Sy Bryant and some of the others. Clint sat with Dodge, Daniels, Charley Smith, and Bob Hatch. All of the horses were picketed and cared for by Manuel who, Clint could tell, knew his way around horses. It showed in the way Eclipse allowed the man to handle him.

Clint walked over while Manuel was rubbing Eclipse down.

"This is a very special horse, señor," Manuel said.

"Yes, he is."

"Magnifico," Manuel said.

"You handle him very well."

Manuel, in his thirties and rail thin, grinned and showed a lot of gold.

"Horses like me, señor."

"I can see that."

"I only wish the wimmins, they liked me as much, eh?" Manuel laughed.

"Manuel, our problem is with the cattle tracks, isn't it?" Clint asked.

"Sí," Manuel said, "I tol' Señor Dodge that the robbers hide their tracks in with the cattle."

"Can you find them again?"

"I try, señor," Manuel said, with a shrug.

"Dodge says you're the best."

Another shrug.

"I do what I can, señor."

"Well, finish up here and come have something to eat at our fire," Clint said.

"Gracias, señor. I will do that."

Clint watched as Eclipse seemed to lean into Manuel's touch, then turned and went back to the fire.

Dodge did, indeed, explain to everyone at the fire what Manuel—and Clint—had noticed. The robbers had hidden their tracks by riding into a herd of cattle.

"Tomorrow we'll split up and try to pick up the trail again. Some of you will go with Manuel, some with me, and others with Clint, who can track pretty well."

It was a surprise to Clint that Dodge considered him a good tracker.

"And we'll set watches for the night by twos," Dodge said. "I'll go and talk to the men at the other fire."

"I'll go with you," Clint offered, standing.

As they walked to the other fire Clint said, "I'll take first watch."

"Okay, good," Dodge said. "I'll put Sy Bryant with you."

"I think I have a better idea," Clint said.

"What's that?"

Clint put his hand on Dodge's arm to stop them before they reached the other fire.

"Pair me up with Heath," Clint said. "I'll see what I can find out."

Fred Dodge grinned at his friend and said, "That is a good idea."

"Yeah," Clint said, as they started walking again, "I get one every now and then."

TEN

Dodge introduced Clint to Heath, and then turned in with the rest of the men.

"We're gettin' started at first light," Dodge said to Clint, "for real, this time."

"I'll be ready."

Clint poured himself a cup of coffee from the second fire, then poured one for Heath.

"Thanks."

"Guess this wasn't exactly what you expected when you came to Bisbee, huh?"

"Whataya mean?"

John Heath was in his late thirties, had the soft-looking hands of a man who had never worked fence posts. Clint had noticed, however, that the man was a good rider.

"Oh, I heard that you run a saloon," Clint said. "I was just thinking you didn't expect to find yourself as part of a posse."

"Hey, if I live in a town, I pitch in," Heath said. "That means volunteerin' for posses."

"Well then," Clint said, "I didn't mean any offense. There should be more town citizens like you."

"You're damn right," Heath said. "I'm gonna walk around a bit."

"I wouldn't do that."

"Why not?"

"You might walk over some tracks in the dark, wipe them out," Clint said. "Manuel's got to have something to read in the morning."

"I know what I'm doin', Adams," Heath said. "I ain't no tenderfoot."

Heath walked off. Clint thought about following him, but it really didn't matter. There wouldn't be any tracks for him to trample. If there were, Manuel would have read them already.

Clint poured some more coffee and sat down by the first fire. When Heath came back he made a point of sitting at the second fire. Clint figured he wasn't going to get any conversation out of him.

But he felt that Dodge was right. There was something wrong with Heath, but he couldn't put his finger on it. He didn't talk like a saloon owner. His reason for being in Bisbee had nothing to do with whiskey and saloon girls.

They got through the night with no trouble. Dodge used the tip of his boot to shake Clint, who came awake immediately. He got up and accepted a cup of coffee from Dodge.

"We ain't got much for breakfast," Dodge said, although Clint detected the smell of bacon in the air. "We're traveling light."

Clint walked to the fire and accepted a few slices of bacon to go with his coffee. At the other fire the posse members were hunkered around the fire, having their breakfast. A couple of men were feeding the horses.

After their hasty meal, they all saddled their own mounts and got ready for the day.

Dodge gathered all the men and broke them into three groups. He, Manuel, and Clint would do the tracking, trying to find the robbers' trail again.

"We're looking for tracks with shoes in among the cattle tracks," Dodge said. "So if anybody thinks they spotted somethin', sing out."

They broke into their three groups. Heath rode with Sy Bryant and Manuel. Dodge told Bryant to keep a close watch on Heath, and at the first sign that he was trying to throw them off the trail, to arrest him and take him back to Tombstone.

Later in the day Manuel rode up on Dodge and told him Heath was trying to throw the trail.

Still later Bryant came by and told him the same thing.

"I think he was wiping out some tracks with his boots," Bryant said.

"First time you can prove it, go ahead and make the arrest," Dodge told him.

In the afternoon Clint's group crossed Dodge's group, and Dodge told him about Heath. At that moment they noticed Manuel's men collected in a group. Dodge pulled out his spyglass and watched as Bryant took John Heath's guns from him. Moments later, two men left to take Heath back to Tombstone.

The groups got together, and Bryant told them what had happened.

"I watched him," he said. "Heath got off his horse and started to deliberately obliterate tracks with his boot. I throwed down on him and arrested him."

"So did we find their trail again?" Dodge asked.

"Yeah," Bryant said. "Manuel picked up a three of shod horse tracks."

"Three men headin' north," Manuel said, pointing.

"Then lead the way," Dodge said.

ELEVEN

They followed the three tracks until they crossed the tracks of two men heading south. Those two appeared to be headed for Sonora.

"Sy, you take your men and half of Manuel's and follow those two. I'll keep goin' north with Manuel, Clint, Bob and Charley Smith, and Bill Daniels," Dodge said. "You catch up to somebody, take them right to Tombstone. We'll meet up there."

"Okay," Bryant said. "The trail is clear enough for me to follow."

Bryant took his men north. Clint, Dodge, Smith, Hatch, Manuel, and Daniels headed north, with Manuel following the trail.

The next night Charley Smith became ill. It was an old wound he had collected in Texas. He'd been shot in the right side of the chest, just below his nipple, and he took cold that night. By morning he was shivering and feverish.

"I have friends who live near here, señor," Manuel said. "If we bring him there they will care for him."

"All right," Dodge said, "let's do it."

Once again Manuel led the way to a ranch house. It was well built and expensive. The people were obviously very well off. They were happy to see Manuel, and very willing to look after Charley, who spoke Spanish and was able to converse with them.

"I'm sorry, Fred," Charley said, as the people took him inside.

"Don't worry about it, pard," Dodge said. "You just get well and meet us in Tombstone."

"I'll do it."

They got back on the trail and then camped for the night. They were now down to five—Dodge, Daniels, Manuel, Hatch, and Clint.

They sat around the fire, shared bacon and coffee, rationing it out. Some of the supplies had gone south with Bryant's group.

"Our numbers are dwindling," Bill Daniels said.

"We've still got enough to do the job," Dodge said.

"Maybe the others are getting some names from Heath," Clint said, "back in Tombstone."

"Maybe we should've asked him before he left," Daniels said.

"Names wouldn't help us track them," Dodge said, although he realized it was a mistake not to have asked Heath the question before he was taken back.

"Can't argue with the decision now," Clint said. "We just have to live with it."

"I'll take the first watch," Dodge said, standing up.

"We'll go every two hours. Clint, you can go last tonight."

"Suits me," Clint said. He finished his coffee and retired to his bedroll.

It was Manuel who woke him with two hours to go before daylight.

"I have made a fresh pot of coffee, señor," Manuel said.

"Good, thanks, Manuel," Clint said.

"Señor?"

"Yes?"

"Señor Dodge should not be so hard on himself, *es verdad*?"

"Yes, it is true, Manuel," Clint said. "He's done nothing wrong that I can see."

"Sí, señor," Manuel said. "That is what I was thinking. He is your amigo, no?"

"Yes, he is my very good amigo."

"He is my amigo, too," Manuel said, proudly. "He has been very good to me. He treats me—how do you say?—with respect."

"Well, you have a talent, Manuel," Clint said, "and he recognizes that."

"Sí, señor," Manuel said. "I am grateful to him."

"You better get some sleep, Manuel," Clint said. "You're going to have to put your talent to good use tomorrow."

"Gracias, señor," Manuel said. "I will see you in two hours."

"Okay, Manuel," Clint said.

As the tracker settled into his bedroll Clint hoped that

Dodge wasn't second-guessing himself too much. The posse had been put together quickly, hoping the robbers would not get too far ahead. Stopping to question Heath would have given them more time. It was more important to stay on their trail.

He went to the fire, poured himself a cup of coffee, and watched the sky, waiting for first light.

TWELVE

Early the next day they came to a split in the trail. One man was heading for the Minas Prietas Mine and the other for the Sierra Madre Mountains.

"Bob, why don't you and Bill take the trail to the Minas Prietas. Clint, Manuel and me, we'll take the wandering trail toward the Sierra Madres." They agreed to return to this point as soon as possible, and agreed upon a signal for each other. If the sign was not there, then those men would take the trail of the others, to give them help.

They followed the trail all day, camped, and took it up again the next day. Late that second day they lost the trail in a creek.

"Can you get it back?" Dodge asked Manuel.

"We will have to ride along the creek both ways to see where he came out, señor," Manuel said.

"Okay," Dodge said. "I'll go with you. Clint, you follow the creek upstream."

"Right."

They split up. Clint rode as far as he dared and never came upon tracks leading out of the creek. When he returned to where they had parted company Dodge and Manuel were already standing there, looking glum.

"No sign?" Dodge asked.

"No."

"Damn it!" Dodge snapped. "We lost him!"

"Easy, Fred," Clint said. "We'll just keep looking."

"I am sorry, Señor Dodge," Manuel said, very contritely.

Dodge put his hand on Manuel's arm and said, "It's not your fault, Manuel. Clint's right. Come on, we'll just keep looking."

They kept looking for almost a week before they found some hope just over the border in Mexico.

Manuel had friends among the Mexican Indians in the Sierra Madres. They came upon a lone Mexican Indian who was able to give them a description of the man they were trailing. The man had come upon a number of Indians—including this one—and had asked for food. The Indians had helped him, and when he gave the description Dodge immediately knew that it was Jack Dowd.

"I knew it," he said. "I can't figure it, but I knew it was him."

Manuel told them that the Indian said Dowd had traded his worn horse for a fresh one.

"At least we know who we're lookin' for, now," Dodge said, slapping Manuel on the back.

*   *   *

Dodge came down with a bad cold for three days that
kept him out of the saddle. Manuel and Clint left him
camped alone and continued to search for some sign of
Jack Dowd. Manuel was still checking with the friendly
Yaquis, and eventually came up with another vital piece
of information. He and Clint rode back to where they'd
left Dodge and found him doing much better.

"Damn cold had settled in my chest and I couldn't
breathe," Dodge said, "but I'm okay, now." He handed
them each a cup of coffee. "What'd you find out?"

"There is a mine about fifteen miles from here," Manuel said.

"It's owned by Mexicans, and there are about twenty-
five or thirty peons working there," Clint said. "Manuel's
friend said they've seen a gringo come in there for supplies a couple of times. The description matches Dowd."

"So he's still in these mountains," Dodge said. "Good.
Manuel, we're headin' for that mine."

THIRTEEN

They stopped outside the mine, which turned out to be more like a small town than a mine.

"Manuel," Dodge said, "Clint and me'll wait up here while you go down and talk to your friend. See if you can find out where Dowd is. If not that, when he might be coming back. And find a place where we can hide."

"Sí, señor."

Manuel rode down into the small town that had been built up around the mine.

"If Dowd is holing up somewhere in these mountains then he's comin' here for supplies," Dodge said. "If Manuel can find a place for us to hide out, we can wait for him to come in and then grab him."

"Unless these people are helping him," Clint said.

"If they are it's probably because he's payin' them," Dodge said.

"That's a strong motive," Clint said.

"We're the law," Dodge said.

"Well, you are," Clint said.

"I am, and they'll do what's right."

"I hope you're right, Fred."

"Relax," Dodge said. "Manuel won't be back for a while."

They made a cold camp and ate beef jerky while they waited.

Manuel returned within half an hour.

"He is staying somewhere in the mountains," Manuel said. "He has been here two times for supplies."

"When will he be coming back?" Dodge asked.

"Two or three days, my friend figures."

"Okay," Dodge said. "Does he have a place for us to wait?"

"Sí, señor. We may wait, and he will feed us."

Dodge looked at Clint. "Sounds good to me," he said.

"Me, too," Clint said. "I could use some hot food."

"They have everythin' we need here, señor," Manuel said. "Food, whiskey . . . and the wimmins."

"Like I said," Clint replied. "This sounds like a place we could sit and wait in comfort."

"Let's go, Manuel," Dodge said.

"Sí, señor," Manuel said. "They are cookin' the food for us now."

They mounted up and rode into town.

FOURTEEN

Manuel had been telling the truth about "the wimmins." There were thirty men working the mines. The rest of the men and women ran the town, and saw to the needs of their guests—paying guests.

But because Manuel was friends with one of them, he, Dodge, and Clint were catered to for free.

"I told you," Dodge said. "Once they saw I was the law they would go along with us."

They were sitting at a table in the house of Manuel's friend, eating enchiladas and beans for supper, and drinking whiskey. There was no beer available.

"They're helping us because of Manuel," Clint said, "not you."

"What does it matter what the reasons are?" Dodge asked.

"You're right," Clint said. "As long as they help us."

"Sí," Manuel said, eating happily and eyeing the two young women who were bringing them the food.

The women were, in turn, eyeing Dodge and Clint.

"Manuel," Clint said, looking at the woman with the big breasts bouncing around inside her peasant blouse, "are either of these women your friend's wife?"

"No, señor," Manuel said, "no wife."

"Daughters?"

"No, señor," Manuel said, with a smile, "no daughters, either."

"Then . . . what?"

Manuel grinned and said, "Seesters. They are his seesters, señor."

"Oh."

The girl with the big breasts leaned over Clint so that he could feel the weight of her on his back and filled his plate with more enchiladas. He looked up at her. This close he could see how pretty she was. She had to be about twenty-five.

The other girl was slender, and younger by a few years. She seemed interested in Dodge, but the lawman was not showing anything in return. Dodge was a handsome man, a double—in fact—for Morgan Earp. It was natural he would attract women, but Fred Dodge always seemed to be more interested in his work.

When the younger girl saw that Dodge wasn't interested, she turned her attention to Manuel, who was only too happy to return the interest.

Dodge told Clint to get some rest after they ate.

"I'll take the first watch, Manuel can go second. We might as well go in four-hour shifts, twenty-four hours a day until we nab him."

"Suits me," Clint said. "Where are we sleeping?"

"Manuel will show you," Dodge said. "I think they're puttin' us in different houses."

Dodge went out to find a good place for them to watch from. Manuel came over to Clint and said, "Señor, you will sleep here."

"Here?" Clint looked around.

"In this house," Manuel said. "This is where Luisa lives. I will be next door, in her sister's house." The man smiled broadly, showing that he was happy with the arrangements.

"Well . . . okay . . ."

"She will be right here to show you to your room," Manuel said. "I will come and get you when it is your watch."

"That'll be in eight hours," Clint said. "I don't think I'll be sleeping that long."

"We will see, señor."

Manuel left and Clint finished his coffee, waiting for Luisa to show him to his room. Luisa's brother—Clint didn't know his name—was nowhere in sight as the girl came out of the kitchen.

"Señor?"

"Are you Luisa?" he asked, staring at her big, round breasts.

"Sí, señor. You will be sleeping in my bed." She put her hand out to him. "Come."

He took her hand and stood up, allowed himself to be tugged along to her room. It was small, but very clean, and the bed looked good to him after all the time on the trail.

"Is this good for you, señor?" she asked.

"It's fine, Luisa," he said. "Thank you."

"If you leave your clothes outside the door I will wash them for you."

"I'll need them back as soon as possible," he said.

"Sí, señor," she said, "that will not be a problem."

She stared at him, as if expecting him to take his clothes off right there and then, and he stared back.

"I'll leave the clothes outside the door, like you said," he told her.

"There is some water there, in the pitcher, señor," she said, indicating the pitcher on the dresser, next to a basin.

"Thank you, Luisa."

"Is there anything else I can do for you, señor?" she asked.

"You've given me your bed, Luisa," Clint said. "What more can I ask?"

"Señor," she said, with a slight bow, and backed out of the room.

Clint went to the bed, pulled the blanket down. The sheets smelled fresh and clean. He undressed to his underwear, put his clothes just outside the door. As a last thought he removed the underwear and put them outside, as well. No point sleeping on clean sheets with dirty underwear.

He went to the pitcher and basin next, poured some water from one into the other. Luisa had supplied a cloth, as well, and he wet the cloth and used it to clean himself from head to toe, including all his crevices. By the time he was done cleaning his genitals he had an erection, probably because he'd been thinking about Luisa the whole time. He stopped before something embarrassing happened, dried himself, then crawled between the sheets.

He fell asleep in seconds.

FIFTEEN

Luisa's younger sister was named Victoria, and she was much more aggressive than her sister. She showed Manuel to her room, and as they entered she reached between his legs and grabbed him.

"Dios mío!" he said, grinning. "You do not play games."

"I know what I want, Manuel," she said. She was wearing a simple dress, rather than the peasant blouse and skirt her sister favored. With a shrug she dropped the dress the ground. She was sleek, where her sister was round. Small breasts, slim hips, smooth skin, and she smelled ready. Manuel could see the dark hair between her legs glistening with moisture.

Well, he was ready, too. He quickly removed his boots, trousers, and shirt, and as his erection sprang into view Victoria was on him, dragging him down onto the bed and mounting him.

From that point there was so much grunting and groan-

ing going on that someone outside the room might think
there was a fight going on inside.

Clint didn't know how much later it was, but he woke to
see Luisa slipping into the room, carrying his clothes in
a bundle. He was lying on his back. He closed his eyes
and pretended to be asleep, but he could feel her looking
at him from across the room, and his body responded. In
moments his penis was erect, hidden by the sheet that
was covering him—but not really hidden.

Eyes still closed he listened for Luisa to leave, but
from the sound of it she wasn't leaving. He heard her
moving, though, and suddenly her breathing—rapid
breathing—was right next to the bed. He debated open-
ing his eyes, but suddenly she was touching him through
the sheet, running her hand up and down the length
of his hard penis. He wondered what would happen
if he did open his eyes. Would she stop? Run out of
the room? His body didn't want her to do either of those
things.

So he kept his eyes closed, even as she grasped the top
of the sheet and peeled it down until it was around his
ankles. She made a sound like "Um," and then he felt
her fingers on his cock. She slid her fingertips along the
underside, making the organ jump on its own. He felt
something on the bed—a knee? Elbow?—and then her
tongue was on him.

He moaned and opened his eyes just as she took him
fully into her hot mouth. He reached down and cupped
her head with his hands.

"I have awakened you?" she asked, after releasing him from her mouth.

"You have," he said.

"You would like me to leave?"

"I would not."

She smiled, stood straight up. He watched as she removed first her blouse, then her skirt. She was naked beneath. Her big breasts swayed as she kicked away the skirt, and then she was in the bed with him. She took his hard cock between her big breasts, letting him fuck her between them. She kissed his chest, his stomach, then pressed her breasts against his thighs as she once again took him into her mouth. Her puffy nipples felt like hard little nubs on his skin. Her wet tongue felt like silk.

She sucked him wetly for some time, as he swelled until he thought he would explode. She released him, then climbed astride him and sank down on him, taking him inside. The heat was molten and he groaned as she began to ride him.

The movements of her breasts fascinated him. They bobbled as she rode him up and down, the dark brown nipples dancing in front of his eyes. She had her head back, her eyes tightly shut, and she was biting her bottom lip to keep from crying out. Her nostrils flared each time she came down on him, and at times she almost snorted.

He brought his hips up to meet her every thrust, still keeping his eyes on those nipples, as if hypnotized by their movements.

Finally, the heat built up inside of him until he couldn't

control it. As he exploded into her she cried out and
he grunted aloud. She sprawled on top of him and he
held her tightly, her pillowy breasts mashed between
them . . .

Dodge had found a place in front of an abandoned building. It kept him hidden from anyone riding into town
from the trail to the north. He might be seen from the
south, but as long as he kept his badge beneath his vest
he didn't think he'd attract attention.

Manuel relieved Dodge, who told him, "Nothing—
haven't seen a soul ride in."

"I have been told not many riders come here," Manuel said.

"That must be why they appreciated Dowd's money,"
Dodge said. "Where's Clint?"

"He is in Luisa's house." Even though Manuel had
heard sounds that led him to believe otherwise he added,
"I believe he is asleep."

"Where am I sleeping?"

"Come," Manuel said. They walked a distance and then
he pointed. "That house belongs to a man named Arturo
Vasquez. He had an extra room. Just tell him who you
are, señor. When he sees your badge he will do what he
can for you."

"Okay," Dodge said. "Thanks. I'll see you later."

"Sí, señor."

"If you see Dowd," Dodge said, "don't try to take
him yourself. Come and fetch me and Clint. Savvy?"

"Sí, señor, I understand."

"Good, good," Dodge said. "We've been after this man

for a long time now. I want to make sure we take him alive and bring him back."

"Sí, señor."

Dodge walked to the home of Arturo Vasquez, and was immediately shown to a comfortable bed.

SIXTEEN

Clint buried his face between Luisa's bountiful breasts, inhaled the scent of her skin, and the musk of her sweat. He licked beads of perspiration from her, and found them sweet and salty.

Luisa was on her back, her chubby thighs open to Clint. He nuzzled her breasts, bit her nipples, while he slid his hand down between her legs to cup her bushy black mound.

"Oh, *dios*," she said, as his fingers delved into the hair and found her wet and slick. He glided his fingers along her wet slit and she caught her breath. He slid one finger inside of her, and then a second. She tensed, then relaxed with a contented sigh.

He couldn't pull himself away from her breasts for some time. This was his favorite part of a woman's body, and Luisa had wonderfully full, heavy ripe breasts with large, brown nipples. He finally had to leave her nipples because he was afraid she'd be too sore to wear her blouse the next day.

He moved down her body, then, kissing her belly, her thighs, rubbing his face along her smooth skin, moving closer and closer to her wet, fragrant pussy. Finally, he removed his fingers and pressed his tongue to her, tasting her, and she jumped and gasped. He began to lick her avidly, lapping up her sweet-salty juices and driving her into a frenzy of passion that went on and on and on, leaving her shaken and exhausted . . .

But he wasn't done with her. Not by a long shot. He straddled her and pressed the spongy head of his hard cock against her pussy. She was so sensitive that she gasped again, her eyes going wide, as he drove himself inside of her, and then she was off again, wave after wave of pleasure flowing over and around her, and through her, as he fucked her at a steady pace, his own eyes closed, chasing his own pleasure while she writhed and moaned beneath him . . .

"Señor Clint," she said, breathlessly, "never before have I known such . . . such pleasure."

"You're welcome," he said. "You're quite a woman, too, Luisa."

"Oh, I was not a woman until now," she said. "No man has ever made me feel . . . that!"

He kissed her.

"Then you've been with the wrong men."

"Sí," she said, "I have. Por favor," she added, reaching down and grasping his semierect penis. "Tell me you have come here to be with me and you will never, ever leave."

"I wish I could tell you that, Luisa," Clint said, trying to sound sincere, "but I'm here to make an arrest and then I must leave and take the prisoner back to Tombstone."

"Oh, I know that," she sighed. "I know you cannot stay, so we have no time to waste." She rolled over on top of him.

"Luisa," he said, putting his hands on her majestic butt, "I have to take my turn and go and stand watch for . . ."

"You have time, señor," she said, covering his mouth with hers.

Well, he thought, maybe a few more minutes . . .

But it turned out to be more than a few minutes.

They had to stay there for three more days before Jack Dowd finally showed up. So Clint spent two more frenzied, magnificent nights with Luisa in her bed, so that he could hardly walk straight by the third day.

Manuel seemed to be having the same problem. Both sisters—though physically very different—seemed to be similarly insatiable in bed.

"I hope Señor Dowd comes soon," Manuel said to him that morning, "or I will not be able to walk straight ever again."

It had become known between them that each was spending the night in the other sister's bed.

"I know what you mean, Manuel."

Manuel smiled and said, "You see what I meant about the wimmins?"

"Oh, yeah," Clint said, "I see."

* * *

It was Dodge himself who was on watch when Jack
Dowd rode into town from the north. Dodge watched the
man ride in and dismount, step inside one of the buildings to do his business.

Dodge broke from cover and ran to get both Clint and
Manuel who, at that moment, were eating in Victoria's
kitchen.

"He's here," Dodge said, bursting into the room. "Just
rode in."

"Where?" Clint asked.

"He dismounted and went into one of the buildings, I
assume, to pick up his supplies."

Manuel's friend was also present, and he quickly
stepped up to warn them.

"Señors, there are those here who do not want you to
take Señor Dowd," he said. "They want his money to
keep coming in."

"Well, his money ain't gonna last much longer,"
Dodge told Manuel's friend. "He's on the run. I'm sure
his money's just about run out."

Clint wasn't so sure of that. He didn't know how
much money Dowd had ended up with from the Bisbee
bank. The robbers might have split the money between
them after they left town.

"I will come with you, señor," the man said. "Perhaps
I can prevent bloodshed. The people listen to me . . .
most of the time."

"Most of the time?" Clint said, looking at Dodge.

"Hopefully," Dodge said, "this'll be one of those
times."

SEVENTEEN

The building Dowd had gone into was like a small trading post. Dodge, Clint, Manuel, and Manuel's friend approached and stopped just outside.

"Do we wait for him to come out?" Manuel asked.

"We could," Dodge said, "but that might encourage some people out here to try to help him."

"Inside's better," Clint said. "It cuts down on his options."

"What about hostages?" Dodge asked.

"Does he know you?" Clint asked.

"On sight, yeah."

"Okay, I'll go in first, see how many other people are in there. I might be able to safeguard them when you walk in. Give me five minutes."

"What if he starts to come out?" Manuel said.

"Then I'll follow him out and we'll brace him there," Clint said. He looked at Dodge. "Okay with you?"

"That's fine. Let's do it."

* * *

Clint walked into the building and was glad to see only two people, the man behind the counter and the fellow who had to be Jack Dowd. Dowd was a big man who looked and smelled as if he'd been in his clothes for a long time. He was wearing a jacket, with his gun belt on the outside, where it was always available. Clint had no idea how good Dowd was with a gun, and didn't want to find out. It would be better to take him without a shot fired.

Clint walked around the small store while Dowd told the clerk what he wanted. He found himself a position where he could see the man from just behind him, only Dowd then noticed him from the corner of his eye and stopped talking.

"Hey, friend?" Dowd said.

"Yeah?" Clint responded. "Are you talking to me?"

"Yeah, I am," Dowd said. "You wanna stand where I can see you?"

"Why's that?"

"I don't like havin' you behind me."

"Hey, friend, I'm just looking around."

Dowd turned to face Clint.

"I'm askin' you to stand where I can see you," he said, his hand hovering near his gun.

"You don't want to do that, Dowd."

Dowd frowned.

"How do you know my name?"

"Just stand easy—"

"I asked you how you know my name."

"Because I told him," Dodge said, from the door.

Dodge stepped in and moved to the right, while Manuel stepped to the left.

"Dodge," Dowd said.

"Take it easy, Jack," Dodge said. "You're comin' back to Tombstone."

Dowd licked his lips. Clint thought there was a look of relief on his face, as if he as glad to see Dodge.

"This fella with you?" he asked, indicating Clint.

"Yeah, he is," Dodge said. "That's Clint Adams."

That shook Dowd.

"Jesus, I almost threw down with the Gunsmith?" he asked. He raised his hands, then. "Take my gun, Dodge."

"Get it, Manuel," Dodge said.

Manuel stepped up, quickly plucked Dowd's gun from his holster.

"Time to head back?" Clint asked.

"We'll talk outside," Dodge said. "Come on, Dowd."

They marched Dowd outside, came face-to-face with about half a dozen armed Mexicans. At the head of them was Manuel's friend.

"I thought you said they listened to you?" Dodge asked.

"They do," the man said, from behind his rifle.

EIGHTEEN

Clint studied the six men. The years had made it easy for him to read men, to see if they were really ready to fire the weapons they were holding. What he saw here were some clerks with guns who weren't ready to go to war.

Clint looked at Manuel's friend, whose name he had never learned.

"What's your name?" he asked. "We never heard."

"I am Armando."

"Armando, you're about to get five men—and maybe yourself—killed, and for what?"

"These are good men," the Mexican insisted.

"I'm sure they are," Clint said, "but Dodge and me, we live by our guns. I guarantee we can put all six of you down, especially with Manuel's help."

"We will get one of you."

"Maybe," Clint said, "but what will that accomplish? The other two will still take Dowd back."

"He has been spending a lot of money here," Armando said. "We need that money."

"Any of you men have wives?"

He saw four of them exchange glances.

"Your wives need you alive more than they need this man's money."

"I'm the law," Dodge said.

"You are not the law here," someone pointed out.

"Good point," Dodge said, "but this man is Clint Adams, the Gunsmith, no matter where we are." He pointed at Clint. "He alone could kill the six of you without reloading."

That got to at least four of the men, who lowered their rifles.

"We are takin' this man back with us," Dodge said. "He is wanted for murder. If all you want is his money, then here." Dodge stepped to Dowd's side and went through his pockets. He came up with some silver, and some paper money. He tossed it on the ground between him and the six men.

"Hey!" Dowd said.

"You're not gonna need it where you're goin', Dowd," Dodge said.

The six men stared at the money on the ground.

"Go ahead, take it," Dodge said.

Armando said something to the other men, who lowered their rifles and walked away. Then he stepped forward and picked up the money.

"We need permission to take this man out of Mexico," Dodge said to Armando. "Where is the *Jefe Politico*?

"He is at the Minas Prietas Mine."

"Do you have a jail?"

"Sí, but it is no good. It would not hold anyone for very long."

"Okay, then we'll go to Minas Prietas," he said. That was where Daniels and the others had gone, anyway.

"You can go," Armando said. "We will not try to stop you again."

"No, you won't," Dodge said, "because next time you won't walk away so easy. Comprende?"

"Sí, señor," Armando said, looking over at Clint. "I understand."

"Get out of here," Dodge said, and Armando walked away.

"That was smart, giving them the money," Clint said.

"Thanks. Manuel?"

"Sí, señor."

"Except for Clint, we need fresh horses."

"Sí, señor," Manuel said. "I will see to it." He looked at Clint. "I will bring your horse, señor."

"Gracias, Manuel."

"We'll wait here," Dodge said. "Sit down, Jack."

Dowd sat down on the steps to the store.

"Think Daniels and the others will still be at Prietas?" Clint asked.

"I hope not," Dodge said. "I hope they found the other men and took them back to Tombstone."

"They probably did," Dowd said. "That's where they went."

"Then you'll be reunited with them in Tombstone,

Dowd," Dodge said. "What was this about, Jack? You been straight since the day I met you. Now you're a god-damned bank robber."

"I needed the money."

"That's it?"

Dowd shrugged. "That's it."

"First bank robbery, and you got caught?"

Dowd shrugged. "I'm ready to go back," he said. "I'm tired of running."

"Well, that's good," Dodge said, looking at Clint, "because I know we're tired of chasing you."

NINETEEN

When they reached the Minas Prietas Mine, Dodge got together with the *Jefe Politico*, with Jack Dowd handcuffed to his left wrist. Clint and Manuel waited outside.

"Señor, I am sorry about Armando," Manuel said. "I did not know."

"It's not your fault, Manuel. Some people change when it comes to money."

"Señor Dodge, he does not blame me?"

"No, he doesn't blame you," Clint said. "Don't worry about it. Everything turned out okay."

"Sí, señor," Manuel said. "Okay."

When Dodge came back out he had permission to remove Dowd from the district and take him back to the United States, and back to Tombstone.

They mounted up and Dodge removed the handcuffs to cuff Dowd's hands together.

"If you try to run," he told the man, "I'll kill you."

"I told you, Dodge," Dowd said, "I'm ready to go back."

"Good," Dodge said. "Manuel, take the lead."

"Sí, señor."

They headed out.

When they reached the trail split where they had parted company, they found Bill Daniels there, sitting on a rock, waiting. He had another man with him, who turned out to be Manuel's brother. He looked relieved to see them coming his way. The two brothers embraced. When Manuel's brother heard from Daniels that Manuel was still in the mountains, he insisted on coming along to find him.

"Been wonderin' where you boys got to," he said. "I see you got Dowd."

They dismounted, shook hands with the deputy.

"How'd you do?" Dodge asked.

"We followed the trail to Minas Prietas and arrested William Delaney there. We took 'im back to Tombstone, and when we got there we found three men in jail already—Tex Howard, Red Sample, and York Kelly."

"You got us all, then," Dowd said. He stood with his hands cuffed in front of him, his head bowed. "Along with John Heath."

"Whataya think?" Dodge asked Daniels.

"Yeah, we got 'em all. They're fixin' to try Heath first off."

"We better get back, then, and let 'em know we got the last one," Dodge said. "Sheriff Ward in town?"

"He is, and folks are sayin' he's got somethin' planned."

"Like what?"

Daniels shrugged.

"Somethin' that'll get him reelected, for sure, they say."

"Ward's a snake," Dodge said. "We better get back before somethin' bad happens."

"Somethin' bad happened when Ward got elected the first time," Daniels pointed out.

"Manuel, you and your brother get Dowd up on his horse," Dodge said.

"Sí, señor."

Dodge turned to Clint.

"What do you think is going to happen?" Clint asked.

"I don't know," Dodge said, "but I wouldn't put nothin' past Jerome Ward—nothin' at all. We better get back quick."

TWENTY

On the way back to Tombstone, Daniels told them the story of how the others had been arrested. Apparently, a colleague of Fred Dodge's in Wells Fargo, the famous lawman J. B. Hume—who Clint also knew—had been instrumental in letting Sheriff Jerome Ward know where the three men were holed up. Hume and a lawman named Tucker had taken in York Kelly, who had given up the names of the other two.

"So somebody else did all the work for Ward," Dodge said, "and he's come in and taken all the credit."

"Pretty much."

Dodge looked at Clint.

"That's just like the man."

Daniels also told Dodge that Charley Smith had come back to town, having recovered from his ailment. At least Dodge was happy about that.

* * *

So when Dodge, Clint, and the others got back to Tombstone with Jack Dowd, that put all of the men responsible for the Bisbee Massacre—York, Howard, Sample, Heath, Delaney, and Dowd—in the Cochise County jailhouse, with Sheriff Ward strutting around with his chest all puffed out.

Clint had decided to stay in town for the trials of all the men. During the trials he found out that the store they had robbed had acted as the Bisbee bank, so it hadn't been hard for them to get hold of the money. They'd killed a lot of people doing it, though, so they were all found guilty and sentenced to hang.

But John Heath had only been found guilty of being an accessory, so he was sentenced to life. The people of Bisbee and Tombstone didn't like that.

But what was done, was done.

Or was it?

Some days later Dodge had to ride out of town to negotiate the return of two six-guns belonging to J. B. Hume. Hume had used the guns in thwarting a stagecoach robbery. Since Clint was the only one who knew that Dodge was also a Wells Fargo man he was asked to go with Dodge, and agreed. So they were out of town for several days.

As they returned to Tombstone they realized immediately that something had happened. Even from a mile and a half away they could see that something was going on.

When they reached town most of the crowd has dispersed, and they saw something hanging from a telegraph pole. By the time they reached it, they could see that it was the body of John Heath. The coroner, Pat Holland, had taken charge and was having the body taken down.

"What happened here, Pat?" Dodge asked.

"Lynch mob," Holland said.

"Who was at the head of it?"

"John Shaunessy."

"No."

"Who's Shaunessy?" Clint asked.

"Foreman of the Grand Central Mine—and I thought, a good friend of mine." Dodge looked at Holland. "You sure?"

"I seen him," the man said.

"Where was Sheriff Ward?"

"Ward made it real easy for them, Fred," Holland said. "The people here and in Bisbee was upset about Heath gettin' off with life. Ward practically gave them the keys to the cell."

Dodge sat back in his saddle.

"This is what he was plannin'," he said to Clint. "Figures by lettin' the townspeople have Heath, he wrapped up the next election."

"And maybe he did," Holland said.

"Not if I have anythin' to say about it," Dodge said.

As they rode into town they could hear the mob celebrating at Pony Brown's Saloon. They left their horses at the livery and walked over to the saloon.

"You don't have to come in with me if you don't wanna," Dodge said.

"You going to try to arrest them?"

"Naw," Dodge said, "can't arrest a whole mob. And if I take Shaunessy in, Ward would probably just let him go."

"So what are you going to do?"

"Give 'em a piece of my mind, I guess."

"I'll back you," Clint said.

"Okay," Dodge said, "let's go."

TWENTY-ONE

When Clint and Dodge entered Pony Brown's, Clint followed his friend right to the bar. There was a table crowded with men who were laughing and pounding one another on the backs. Clint knew this had to be the celebrating mob.

"Two beers," Dodge said to the bartender.

"You hear about—" the barman started, but Dodge cut him off.

"I heard, Ike," Dodge said. "Just bring the two beers, huh?"

"Sure, Fred."

As Ike went off to get the beer, Dodge said to Clint, "Ike Roberts. He's a constable."

"Guess he didn't do anything to stop these fellows, either. That them?"

"Yep," Dodge said. "That's Shaunessy right in the middle of 'em."

"How do you want to play it?"

"Let 'em come to us."

Clint nodded.

Roberts returned with the two beers and set them down in front of them.

"Thanks, Ike."

Suddenly, the men at the table quieted down, as if they noticed Dodge at the bar.

"Hello, Fred," Shaunessy said.

"Hello, John," Dodge said, and nothing else.

He and Clint sipped their beers. Eventually, the men at the table couldn't take the silence anymore.

"Well," Shaunessy finally said, "you boys saw the work. What do you think of it?"

Dodge turned to face the man.

"Yeah, we saw the effects of your work, John."

"Well?" Shaunessy asked. "What did you think of it?"

"You don't want to know what I think, John."

"Yeah, I do," Shaunessy insisted. "Come on, Fred. What do you think?"

"Okay, since you insist," Dodge said. "I think you are all a bunch of no-account, murdering, law-breaking, cowardly scoundrels."

Shaunessy stood up so fast his chair fell over.

"You got no love for John Heath, Fred," he said. "I know that. You got no call—"

"I'm wearin' a badge, John," Dodge said, "and you boys committed murder. I got call."

Shaunessy looked at Clint, then.

"You're Adams, right?"

"That's right."

"Well, whataya think?"

"That goes for me, too, Shaunessy," Clint said. "I'll back Deputy Dodge all the way."

Dodge turned his back and leaned on the bar. Clint followed. Shaunessy stood there for a few moments, then righted his chair and sat down. The mob was quiet.

"What happened, Ike?" Dodge asked.

"Hell, Fred," Roberts said, "couldn't have been more than half a dozen guns on the mob. Will Ward practically left the door open for them."

"That's Ward's son, his jailer," Dodge said.

"It was planned, Fred," Roberts said. "I didn't know nothin' about it."

"I know you didn't, Ike." Dodge dropped some money on the bar.

"Hell, Fred, you're a deputy," Roberts said. "You don't have to pay."

"No, I ain't," Dodge said, "and yeah, I do."

He walked out, Clint following him. The first man they encountered was Sheriff Jerome Ward.

"Jesus, Fred, there you are," Ward said. "A goddamned lynch mob practically killed my son breakin' Heath out and then they hung him—"

Dodge stopped Ward by taking his deputy commission from his pocket, tearing it up and throwing it in the man's face.

"Yeah, I know about it, Ward," Dodge said. "And you're an accessory before and after the fact."

He took his badge off and dropped it at the man's feet.

He walked away.

Ward looked at Clint.

"You're Adams, right?"

"Yes."

"What's wrong with—"

"The law's the law, Ward," Clint said. "If it was me, I would have stuck that badge up your goddamned ass."

He turned and walked away.

As it turned out, the townspeople and the miners didn't appreciate a sheriff who would conspire with a lynch mob.

Ward did not even run in the next election, and Bob Hatch was elected Sheriff.

TWENTY-TWO

TOMBSTONE, ARIZONA TERRITORY
1886

Clint had managed to replay the entire Bisbee Massacre in his head while taking his bath. When he finished, he stepped out, bathed and cleanly shaven, and decided he needed some new duds to go with his otherwise fresh appearance.

He spent some time buying a couple of shirts, some new trousers, socks, and underwear, but stayed with the same hat, which he'd had for some time.

After his shopping he went back to the hotel to his room to change into his new clothes. By then it was about time to go over to the Bird Cage and check it out while waiting for Dodge. And he was looking forward to that steak.

As he entered the Bird Cage he saw that little had changed, but it still felt very different to him. Must have had something to do with Doc Holliday's faro table being tended by someone else. Also, no Wyatt Earp—no Earps at all.

He went to the bar and ordered a beer, looking at himself in the mirror on the wall behind the bartender. He wondered how many famous and infamous men had looked in the same mirror? He also wondered what they saw?

"Passin' through?" the bartender asked. He was young—too young to have been there during the O.K. Corral or the Bisbee Massacre.

It seemed a little busy in the place for the man to want to make conversation.

"Visiting a friend," Clint said. "But I've been here before—many times."

The young bartender nodded, went to wait on some new blood. Clint turned, leaned against the bar, and nursed his beer. There was nothing happening on stage at the moment, but he knew the cribs on the lower level would be full. There were several girls working the floor, and the games were in full swing. He didn't bother looking for an open chair, though. He wouldn't have wanted to be involved in a game when Dodge showed up.

He wondered why Dodge was still with Wells Fargo? He hadn't seen him since 1883, but he had seen Jim Hume a couple of years ago. They had talked about Dodge a bit. Clint wondered how Dodge could keep working undercover, and being a deputy, and being a constable, and keeping all the jobs straight. At least he used the same name for each job. It wasn't like he was undercover using an assumed name. That was the kind of thing his friend Jim West, the Secret Service agent, used to do. West liked it, and kept doing it, so he figured Dodge must have liked what he was doing and was probably still doing it.

Hume was more of a supervisor these days than an agent, and he had a very high opinion of Dodge, as did Clint. He also knew his friend in Denver, Talbot Roper, respected Fred Dodge, as well. It was amazing how the Wells Fargo agents, the Pinkertons, and private detectives, as well as the Secret Service agents all seemed to know one another—or, at least, know of each other. The one man Clint had not heard from in some time was an Irishman named O'Grady, who also worked for the Secret Service. No telling what he as doing, now.

He finished his beer, decided to get a second and nurse it even slower, but at that moment Dodge came walking in. Clint waved to the young bartender and held up two fingers. The man nodded.

"Got a beer coming," Clint said as Dodge joined him at the bar.

"Good, I can use it."

"Still juggling jobs, eh?"

"Most days I enjoy it," Dodge said. "Better than doin' the same exact thing every day."

"But not today?"

"It's been kind of a rough day, and I think it's gonna get rougher."

"How so?"

The beer came and he nodded to the barman. Dodge took a deep drink before answering.

"There are some neighbors outside of town I think are headin' for trouble."

"What kind?"

"The domestic kind," Dodge said.

"Oh, yeah, I think I heard something about that."

"From who?"

"I forgot to tell you I talked to Hatch earlier," Clint said. "He was looking for some fellow named Riggs, I think?"

"Barney and Bannock," Dodge said. "Barney's the younger, and he's married. Seems he thinks his neighbor, fella name of Hudson, has been seein' his wife."

"And has he?"

Dodge rolled his eyes.

"Probably."

"Aren't there enough women in Tombstone without going after somebody's wife?"

"You'd think," Dodge said. "Plenty of women workin' downstairs."

Dodge shook his head and drank his beer.

"That all that's botherin' you?"

"No," Dodge said. "But I'll tell you over a steak. Cattleman's?"

"Sounds good to me."

They both finished their beers and set the empty mugs down on the bar.

"Place looks the same, don't it?" Dodge asked.

"Yeah," Clint said, with a nod, "and yet so different, you know?"

Dodge looked around, then said, "Yeah, I know what you mean."

They left and headed for Cattleman's Steak House.

TWENTY-THREE

When they were situated at a table against a wall with steak dinners in front of them, Dodge said. "It's Bob Hatch."

"Your sheriff? What about him?"

"He's doin' the same thing Barney Riggs's neighbor is doin'," Dodge said.

"With the same woman?"

"No," Dodge said, "with his neighbor's wife."

"Jesus, things sure have changed around here," Clint said. "I'm used to people trying to shoot each other, but all this . . . infidelity."

"I know," Dodge said.

"How do you know about Hatch?"

"He brags," Dodge said. "He has a room at the end of town and he meets her there."

"Is Hatch married?"

"Yes."

"What's he thinking?"

"He ain't thinkin'," Dodge said. "Or maybe he's just thinkin' with his dick."

"A lot of men have gotten in trouble doing that," Clint said.

"Thank God I'm too busy."

"Ah," Clint said, "the perfect reason to have three jobs."

"Well, it keeps me out of this kind of trouble."

"Have you talked to Hatch about it?"

"I have," Dodge said, cutting into his meat. "He brags about it, I told you. He's proud of himself. He's got his wife uptown and his woman downtown."

"Makes him feel powerful," Clint said, chewing a piece of steak.

"Yes!" Dodge said, gesturing with his knife. "That's it. He walks around with his chest all puffed out, like he can do anything."

"Is it affecting his job?"

"I wish I could say it was," Dodge said. "But if it was I wouldn't want to take over. Actually being the sheriff would just get in my way."

"What about Charley?"

"He don't wanna be sheriff, either," Dodge said.

"So nobody wants the job and Hatch does. Let him do it. If he messes it up, let him mess it up."

"I don't care who messes what up," Dodge said. "I just don't want people getting killed."

"I can't blame you for that."

"To tell you the truth, Clint," Dodge said, "I don't know how much longer I can keep this up. I may have to come in from the outside, eventually."

"You mean as a Wells Fargo agent?" Clint said. "Let everybody know?"

"Well, not everybody," Dodge said. "I mean, I won't put it in the newspapers, but I'd carry my credentials and identify myself."

"So no more deputy's badges?"

"No," Dodge said, "just my Wells Fargo badge."

"Do you have it on you?" Clint asked. "I don't think I've ever seen one."

"No," Dodge said, "I don't carry it. I've got it hidden away. It's good-lookin', though. I'll show it to you, some time."

"I'll hold you to that."

They continued to eat and talk and, when they were done, paid their bill and stepped outside. Immediately, someone came running up to Dodge. It was Charley Smith.

"It finally happened, Fred."

"What?"

"Barney Riggs."

"Oh, shit," Dodge said.

"Yep," Charley said, "he killed Hudson."

"Do you know it was him?" Clint asked.

Charley looked at Clint for the first time. His face brightened as he recognized him.

"Hey, Adams. I didn't know you was in town. Um, well, nobody saw him do it, but Riggs ain't exactly the type to brace a man from the front."

"Shot him in the back?" Dodge asked.

"Yup. Snuck up on him."

"Damn. Okay, does Hatch know?"

"Yeah," Charley said, "he sent me after you. He rode out there."

"Okay, I'll ride out, too. Guess you better stay in town and watch things."

"Okay."

"You wanna come?" Dodge asked Clint.

"I wouldn't miss it," Clint said. "A chance to see you and Hatch in action together."

"I don't know," Charley said.

"Know what?" Dodge asked.

Charley gave Clint a sidelong glance.

"You can say what you want in front of Clint, Charley," Dodge said.

"I ain't so sure Bob wants to catch Barney, if you know what I mean, Fred," Charley said.

"Yeah, Charley," Dodge said. "I know what you mean."

TWENTY-FOUR

The two houses were just out of town. They were small ranches, with the main houses actually being walking distance apart. Clint thought this must have made it easy for the cheating couple.

When they rode up to one of the houses Clint knew this was the Hudson house because there was a dead man sprawled on the ground. Standing over him, staring down mournfully, was Sheriff Bob Hatch.

"Glad you brought Clint, Fred," Hatch said, as they approached on foot.

There were some men milling about. Clint assumed they were employees of Hudson.

"This was bound to happen," Hatch said, as Fred leaned over the body. Hatch had no idea Dodge was a trained detective, but he deferred to him, anyway.

"Shot in the back, all right," Dodge said. "Damn it." He stood straight up. "Not much doubt about who did it, Bob."

"We don't have no witnesses, Fred."

"That don't mean we can't hunt him down," Dodge shot back.

"If he's even on the run," Sheriff Hatch said. "What if he's just settin' in his living room with his wife and Pa?"

"Then we'll take him in for questioning," Dodge said. "You wanna go over there together?"

"Sure," Hatch said. "Let's get somebody to throw a blanket over Hudson until the doc gets here."

They waited for one of the hands to bring a blanket over and lay it over his boss.

"Don't let nobody near the body," Hatch told the man. "We're goin' next door to see if Barney's there."

"He ain't gonna be there, Sheriff," the hand said. "He back-shot the boss and lit out."

"Did you see him do it?" Clint asked.

"Well, no—"

"Then keep your opinions to yourself, Sam," Dodge said. "You're the foreman, it's up to you to keep your men in line."

"I understand."

"We'll be right back, probably before the doc even gets here."

"I won't let nobody near him, Dodge."

"Okay."

Dodge, Hatch, and Clint walked over to the Riggs house.

When a woman answered their knock at the door, Clint was taken aback. She was a rare beauty, with long black hair framing a heart-shaped face. Now he knew why Hudson was dipping his wick next door.

"Yes?"

"Sheriff Hatch, Mrs. Riggs. Can we come in? We gotta talk to Barney."

"Barney's not here, Sheriff."

"Where is he?"

"I—I don't know." She lifted her chin defiantly. Clint admired her. She was standing up for a husband who cheated on her.

"Is Bannock here?" Dodge asked.

"My father-in-law is home, yes."

"May we speak to him, ma'am?" Dodge asked.

"Of course," she said. "Come in, gentlemen."

The three men entered, and as the woman closed the door behind them they all removed their hats. The house was small and they could see Bannock Riggs sitting in front of the fireplace. The old man stood up, slightly stooped but still tall.

"What's this all about, Sheriff? Dodge?" He frowned at Clint. "Who's this feller?"

"This is Clint Adams, Bannock," Dodge said. "He's helpin' us with somethin'."

"Somethin' that brung you here, lookin' for my boy?" the man demanded.

"That's right," Dodge said. Hatch seemed satisfied to let Dodge do the talking. "Bannock, somebody killed your neighbor, Hudson."

They heard a slight intake of breath from Mrs. Riggs.

"That's too bad," the old man said. "What's that got to do with us?"

"Come on, Bannock," Dodge said. "You know we got to talk to Barney."

"Barney didn't do nothin'," Bannock said. "Why would Barney kill Hudson?"

With that the three men turned their heads and looked at Mrs. Riggs. She still seemed stunned by the news that her lover was dead.

"Clint," Dodge said, "why don't you take Mrs. Riggs outside while Hatch and I talk to her father-in-law."

"Sure, Fred. Ma'am?"

Clint knew what Dodge was doing. Separating daughter-in-law and father-in-law so they could be questioned separately.

He escorted the lady outside.

TWENTY-FIVE

Outside Mrs. Riggs hugged her upper arms, as if she was cold, but Clint thought she was feeling something else. Maybe guilt? Maybe she was feeling trapped?

"Mrs. Riggs," Clint said, "it's in your husband's best interest for you to tell us where he is. If the law has to track him down he might end up dead."

"Is Hudson really dead?" she asked.

"He is."

"How?"

"Shot in the back."

"And Barney did it?"

"That's what everyone thinks," Clint said. "What do you think?"

She thought a moment, then said, "Yes, I think he did it, too."

"Then will you help me find him?"

"Didn't you say if the law had to track him down he might end up dead?" she asked.

"I did."

"Then let them track him down."

"You don't care if they kill him?"

"No," she said, "I don't care at all."

With that she turned her back on Clint.

"Bannock," Dodge said, "you must know if we have to track Barney down he could end up dead. You don't want that, and we don't want that."

"Why do you think Barney killed Hudson?" Bannock asked.

"You don't know?" Dodge asked.

"No, I don't."

"It's about Hudson and your daughter-in-law, Mr. Riggs," Hatch said.

"What are you talkin' about," Bannock asked. "Linda didn't have nothin' to do with Hudson."

"That might or might not be true," Dodge said, "but the fact is Barney thought there was somethin' goin' on, and that was enough for him to bushwhack Hudson on his own property."

"You say."

"That's right, I say," Dodge said. "Come on, you know me, Bannock. Why would I lie?"

"I ain't sayin' you're lyin'," Bannock Riggs said. "I'm sayin' you're wrong."

"About what?" Hatch asked.

"About everythin'," Bannock said. "While you're blamin' my boy, huntin' him down for somethin' he didn't do, your real killer is gonna get away."

"We got the right man fingered, Mr. Riggs," Hatch said. "It's only a matter of time before we catch him."

"Then you go and catch him."

Hatch and Dodge exchanged a glance, then shrugged.

"We got to search the house, Bannock," Dodge said.

"Go ahead, it won't take you long."

It didn't take long. When they opened the door and stepped outside, Linda Riggs still had her back to Clint.

"Anything?" Dodge asked.

"Not a thing," Clint said. "She doesn't care if you have to kill her husband."

"The old man won't give us a thing," Dodge said.

"We better get to town and gather us up a posse, then," Hatch said.

"Let's see if Doc is over at Hudson's," Dodge said. "He's got to take the body back to town. We might as well ride along with him."

Hatch nodded and the three men headed back to the other house. Linda Riggs watched them go, then turned and walked back inside slowly.

Linda had just closed the door and turned when Bannock Riggs slapped her across the face. She staggered back against the door, bounced off it. He reached out, grasped the front of her dress and tore the garment from her. Full, firm breasts sprang forward with dark nipples already hard.

"You bitch!" he said. He grabbed her bare breasts and twisted them. She yelped in pain. He put both hands on her bare shoulders and pushed her to her knees in front of him, then undid his trousers.

"You been ruttin' with the neighbor, you might as well rut with me."

"W-what about Barney?" she asked.

"Barney ain't here," the old man said. He dropped his pants and his huge penis came into view, already hardening. It had huge veins and a large, bulbous head on it.

"You open your mouth, Missy," he said. "And if you even think about bitin' me, I'll kill ya."

"I'm not gonna bite you, Pa," she said.

She took his penis in both hands, ran her hands up and down it. Then she held it at the base with one hand, and cupped his huge, hanging testicles with the other.

"That's it, gal," he said. "The way I like it."

Bannock Riggs was standing at his full height, not stooping the way he'd been in front of the lawmen.

Linda ran her tongue around the head of her father-in-law's penis, wetting it thoroughly before taking his penis into her mouth and sucking him. She didn't mind sucking the old man's dick. It was better than being with Barney. That was why she had been having sex with Hudson, too. Anything was better than Barney.

"Ahh," the old man said. He dropped his head back, took her head in his hands while she rode him wetly with her mouth. "That's a girl."

She sucked him for a while, and when she knew she had him she let him go and said, "Lie down on your back, Pa."

He did it, right there on the floor. On his back his penis stood straight up. She stood over him, straddled him and took him in her hand, held him firm so she could slide down on him. Then she closed her eyes and began to ride up and down on his rigid pole.

"Shit, gal," he groaned, "ah, shit . . ."

TWENTY-SIX

They all rode back to town with Hudson's body on a buckboard. Hatch dispatched Charley Smith to gather up a posse. Dodge and Clint accompanied the doctor and the body to the undertaker's office. They lifted the body from the buckboard and carried it in.

They left the doctor inside with the undertaker and stepped outside.

"The wife doesn't care if you kill her husband," Clint said. "But I didn't get the feeling it was all because he killed her lover."

"The old man wouldn't help, either," Dodge said. "That's a strange family."

"What do you think the old man will do to his daughter-in-law, for cheating?" Clint asked.

"I don't know," Dodge said. "I didn't think of that. I sure hope he doesn't kill 'er."

"And why would she go back inside?"

"Maybe she's got nowhere else to go."

"No family in town?"

"She's not from here. Barney brought her back here with him one day."

"How long ago?"

"'Bout a year."

"So she doesn't know anybody else in town?"

"She does. But nobody she'd go and stay with," Dodge said. "At least, I don't think so."

"Well, maybe she'd just stay with the old man, then."

"Look, I got to catch up to Charley, put a posse together for tomorrow. You want to ride along?"

"Jesus," Clint said, "last time I said yes I was in the Sierra Madres with you for weeks."

"Yeah, right, Bisbee," Dodge said. "That was the last time we saw each other, right?"

"That's right."

"Well, this shouldn't take weeks," Dodge said. "Why don't you just wait here till I get back? Then we'll really have a few drinks and catch up."

"That sounds good to me, Fred," Clint said. "In fact, I'm going to turn in now."

"I'll be gone by the time you wake up, but stay around, do some gamblin' and some eatin' and whatever else you want to do until we get back with Barney."

"I'll do that," Clint said. "I'll do just that."

Clint was drinking in the Crystal Palace when, to his surprise, Fred Dodge walked in.

"What the hell?" he said. "I thought you were out with the posse."

"Yeah, I thought I was goin' out with the posse, too," he said, signaling the bartender for a beer.

"What happened?"

"Hatch. He told me and Charley to stay in town."

"Why?"

"Because he's the boss, that's why."

"He's not half the lawman you are."

"I know that, but he is the sheriff."

"Why would he want to go after Riggs without you and Charley?"

"Maybe he wants all the credit," Dodge said. "I don't know."

"Well, look at the bright side," Clint said.

"What's that?"

"You and me aren't riding around the mountains for weeks."

Dodge clinked his mug with Clint's and said, "I'll drink to that."

TWENTY-SEVEN

Clint rolled over and bumped into an impressive pair of breasts. He bounced off, opened his eyes, and stared at the pink nipples. They sat pertly atop a pair of lovely, full, heavy, pale-skinned breasts.

The girl's name was Angel. She was blond and buxom, in her twenties. She worked the floor of the Bird Cage, but not the cribs. She was a saloon girl, but not a whore, and she was in Clint's bed because she wanted to be.

He watched as she slept, wondrous chest rising and falling with every breath.

She opened her sky blue eyes, and he was again startled by them, as he had been the first night they met, five days ago.

"Good morning," she said.

"Morning," he said. He leaned over and kissed her mouth. "Sorry I bumped into you."

She reached down beneath the sheet and grabbed hold of his rigid penis.

"No, you're not sorry at all," she said, stroking him gently.

He smiled and said, "No, I'm not."

He grabbed her and this time kissed her soundly. She returned the kiss with eagerness, her tongue blossoming in his mouth.

She went beneath the sheet and took his cock in her mouth. He threw the sheet back so he could watch as she sucked him. She wet him thoroughly, so much so that at one point she was almost slurping. He settled back to enjoy her attention, but he was quickly becoming excited and didn't want it to end too quickly.

He grabbed her by the hair and pulled her off him. She laughed as he yanked her up onto him, and wriggled as he tried to poke her. After she'd teased him enough she allowed him to pierce her, and caught her breath as he filled her.

"Oooh, ohh," she said, sitting up on him and riding him. He watched as her breasts bounced and bobbed. He grabbed them, then, so he could bite her nipples as she rode him.

"Oh, yeah," she said, "harder, bite me harder, come on . . ." She began to ride up and down on him harder, so that when she came down on him there was an audible slap of flesh on flesh. For a sweet-looking blonde, she liked her sex hard.

They were grunting as she hopped up and down on his cock. He could feel her gushing on him, soaking them both, and the sheet beneath them. He had only encountered a few women in his time who did this. She almost . . . squirted when she became too excited, but she kept going and going . . . until it happened again and again . . .

He rolled her over, found a dry place on the bed, lifted her legs into the air by linking his arms beneath her meaty thighs. He fucked her that way until the bed was once again wet beneath them. Finally, he exploded into her with a loud shout, then rolled off her.

"Thank God," he said.

She laughed, rolled away and sat on the side of the bed, her feet on the floor.

"We could've drowned," she said, laughing.

It was no laughing matter. The first time she had . . . squirted . . . he'd been working on her with his mouth and tongue. He thought he would drown until he turned his head away.

"How do you do that?" he asked her, now.

"I don't know," she said. "It just . . . happens when I get excited. I used to be really embarrassed by it, but . . . well, I guess you didn't mind after the first time, did you?"

"No," he said. "I didn't mind. I find it . . . pretty fascinating."

"Exciting?" she asked, looking at him over her shoulder.

"Everything about you is exciting, Angel," he said. "Your eyes, your beautiful skin, your breasts . . . all of it. I saw that the first time I saw you."

She hadn't been on the floor of the Bird Cage his first time in there, but after he and Dodge had gone there the night the posse left he spotted her right away. Now, five days later, she'd been to his room three nights in a row. The first night they were together had been in her room.

"You're a sweet man," she said, "but having sex with you has another effect on me."

"What's that?"

"It makes me hungry. Breakfast?"

As they entered the café they saw Fred Dodge sitting alone at a table, drinking coffee and either waiting to order, or waiting for his order to be delivered to his table. He spotted them and waved them over.

"Do you mind?" Clint asked her.

"No, I like Fred," she said, "but thank you for being a gentleman and asking."

"Come and join me," Dodge invited as they reached his table, "that is, if I wouldn't be intruding on the two of you?"

"Not at all," Clint said. "We're here to eat."

She sat down and smiled at Dodge.

"Good morning, Deputy."

"Good morning, Miss Angel."

A waitress came with a plate of steak and eggs for Dodge. It looked good, and Clint ordered the same for both himself and Angel.

"Any word?" Clint asked Dodge.

"Yeah, I've got word," Dodge said. "Hatch can't find him. Or won't."

"What's that mean?"

"It means somebody else has to go out and look for him."

"Like who?"

"Charley Smith knows Barney Riggs and his wife," Dodge said. "He thinks he knows how to find him."

"So the two of you want to go out?"

"Maybe," Dodge said, "the three of us?"

"With Hatch's okay?"

"If Hatch won't find Riggs, then maybe we shouldn't tell him that we're gonna do it," Dodge said. "Charley's got some time off comin'. He's gonna ask for it, leave town, and then meet up with us."

"Then what?"

"Then it's up to Charley," Dodge said. "We'll just go along to back him up. It's his play. When we make the catch, it'll be his."

"That's fine with me," Clint said.

Angel was eating while they talked, watching both of them intently.

"That looks good," Clint said to her.

"It is," she said. "You should stop talking and start eating."

Dodge grinned at Clint.

"I think the little lady makes a good point," Dodge said.

He and Clint dug in.

TWENTY-EIGHT

Clint met Dodge at the livery stable. They saddled their horses.

"Charley left earlier," Dodge told Clint.

"Where did you tell Hatch you were going?" Clint asked.

"I told him I had some people to see in Bisbee," Dodge said.

"People?"

"He doesn't care," Dodge said. "But I need to saddle Charley's horse."

"Charley? I thought he left earlier?"

"He did, by stage. We'll have to meet up with him at Dragoon Summit."

"Dragoon Summit? Where's that?"

"The other side of the Riggs place. There's a railroad stop there. That's where Charley's gonna meet us."

"Then what?"

"He's gonna take us to a spot not far from the Riggs

place. We'll have water and feed for the horses, and through field glasses we'll be able to watch the Riggs house."

"That's Charley's plan?" Clint asked. "Watch the house?"

"Watch the woman."

"Riggs's wife? I thought she hated him? Didn't care if he was killed?"

"Or that's what she wanted us to think."

"So she was cheating on him, but she'll help him escape capture for killing her lover?"

Dodge looked at Clint, shrugged, and said, "Women."

It took them half the day to get to Dragoon Summit. They had to actually ride past the Riggs place to get to it—and they circled it so that they wouldn't be seen.

When they got to Dragoon Summit, Charley Smith was already there. He was waiting for them on the train platform. When he saw them he stepped down and came forward to accept the reins of his horse from Dodge.

"Glad you're here, Clint," he said.

"Didn't have anything more interesting to do," Clint replied.

Charley mounted up and took the lead.

He led them to a clearing above and behind the Riggs place. As Dodge had said, the horses could stand and feed while they waited. As for the men, they had beef jerky, and plenty of water.

Dodge pulled his field glasses out of his saddlebags and trained them on the Riggs house.

"Nice and clear," he said. "I'll be able to see the hairs on his face."

"What's the story here, Charley?" Clint asked the deputy.

"I know Barney and Linda Riggs pretty well," Charley said. "It don't matter what they do to each other, they love each other. In fact, throw in the old man, the whole family's close. Whatever happened, they'd try to help each other."

"So you think the wife or the old man is going to meet up with Barney?"

"I'm bettin' on it," Charley said. "In fact, maybe Barney'll just come home."

Clint turned to Dodge, who was still looking down at the house.

"Hatch didn't think to have someone watch the house?" he asked.

"No, he didn't," Dodge said. "There are a lot of things Hatch doesn't think of."

"Sounds to me like you were right," Clint said.

"Right about what?" Charley asked.

"Sounds like Hatch doesn't really want to find Barney Riggs."

Dodge didn't answer. Clint walked over and sat on a rock next to Charley Smith, who handed him a hunk of beef jerky.

"Thanks. So what do you think, Charley?" he asked, taking a bite.

"About what, exactly?" Charley replied. "The murder? I think Barney did it, all right. He was mighty jealous of Hudson."

"Then why would he expect his wife to help him?" Clint asked.

"I told you. They're close."

"It doesn't make sense to me."

"The whole family is mighty close," Charley said again. He stared directly at Clint. "She's close to old Bannock Riggs, too. Understand?"

Clint stared at Charley.

"You mean—"

"That's what I mean."

"But . . . why?"

"Barney and old Bannock share everything."

"Even the son's wife?"

"Everything," Charley said. "That's the way they are."

"So then, why is it so obvious that Barney killed Hudson?" Clint asked. "Why not the old man?"

"Because Bannock didn't care about Linda that way," Charley said.

"So Barney didn't mind sharing her with his father, but not with anybody else."

"Right."

"And the old man, he'd share her with anyone?"

"Right again."

"So he'd have no reason to kill Hudson."

Charley nodded.

"And Barney would," he said.

"She could have walked away with us that night," Clint said. "Away from the old man. Why didn't she?"

"That's an easy one," Charley said. "She didn't want to."

TWENTY-NINE

It was Clint's turn at the glasses. He couldn't understand women who stayed with men who were abusive to them. And sharing your wife with your father qualified as abuse, to him. Maybe the neighbor, Hudson, was nice to her, but if he was why would she want to help her husband get away with killing him?

He didn't understand women, but maybe Charley Smith did.

Finally, in the afternoon, Mrs. Riggs—or "Mrs. Barney," as Dodge called her—came out with a spyglass of her own. She put it to her eye and looked up at a hill that was opposite the position where Clint and his companions were. Clint moved his glasses to that hill and he saw a flash of light—a signal.

"We got him," he said.

The others joined him.

"Where?" Dodge said.

"Up on that hill," Clint said. "There was a flash of light to signal her."

They all looked down at the house. Mrs. Barney had already gone back inside.

"Two choices," Dodge said. "We can go over there now and look for him, or wait for her and follow her."

"I say we follow her," Charley said. "She'll probably go and meet him after dark."

Dodge looked at Clint.

"Sounds good to me."

"Okay," Dodge said, "so we keep takin' turns watchin' her. Maybe the old man will even go with her."

"Any chance Riggs has somebody with him?" Clint asked.

"Can't think who it would be," Charley said. "Him and ol' Bannock keep to themselves."

"Okay," Dodge said. "It's gettin' dark. We'll keep a cold camp and watch."

The others went back to their former position and Clint lifted the field glasses to his eyes again.

It wasn't until just before sunset that light came from the open door of the house. In that light Clint saw Mrs. Barney Riggs come out of the house. She went to the barn and came out with a saddled horse. She walked back to the house and the door opened again. Old Man Bannock came out and handed her a bunch of supplies, which she tied to her saddle.

She mounted, then, and headed for that hill where Clint had seen the flash of light.

"Time to go!" Charley said. He had relieved Clint of the glasses a couple of hours before.

Their horses were still saddled so they only had to mount up and ride out, keeping the woman in sight.

They decided that Charley would track her alone, just in case she was able to hear their horses behind her. Clint and Dodge rode well behind Charley, tracking him rather than her.

As they approached the hill it became obvious that Mrs. Barney was heading right for the spot on the hill Clint had seen the flash of light. Charley rode back to Clint and Dodge to let them know.

"I know a place we can watch from," he added. "We just have to circle, but we should be there before her."

"Are you sure?" Dodge asked

"I'm sure, Fred," Charley said.

"Okay," Dodge said. "This is your catch. We'll follow your lead."

They followed Charley to a certain point where he called for them to dismount and leave their horses. They'd be traveling over rocks from this point on and the horses' hooves would make too much noise.

They crept along, closer to where Charley wanted them to be, and when they got there they all got down on their chests and watched. Charley had been right on the money, for they were mere feet away from where Mrs. Barney Riggs was now waiting.

Like them, she had left her horse behind and advanced on foot. Before long, and as the sun started to go down, Barney Riggs appeared and approached her. The husband and wife did not embrace, but they fell into a rapid conversation they were not going to finish.

Charley got to his feet then and moved in on them. Clint and Dodge followed, but they were only backing him up.

"All right, Barney, throw your hands in the air, partner," Charley Smith said, gun in hand.

Barney gave his wife a murderous look, as if he suspected her of leading the law there on purpose.

"Take it easy, Barney," Charley said. "She didn't know nothin' about it. I just decided we should follow her."

"Charley," Barney said, "you wouldn't shoot me, would you?"

"I'm wearin' a badge, Barney," Charley Smith said. "It's my job to shoot you if you try to escape. And if I don't do it, one of these fellas will."

Barney looked past Charley at Dodge and Clint.

"Damn it, Charley, he deserved it—"

"Don't admit to anythin' we'll have to swear to in court, Barney," Dodge said, quickly. "Just come along quietly."

Clint moved in, relieved Barney of a rifle and a six-shooter, and then took the six-shooter Linda Riggs was wearing.

"What were you going to do with this, ma'am?" Clint asked.

She just stared at him.

"I'll take Mrs. Riggs to her horse," Dodge offered.

"Fine," Charley said. "Me and Clint'll walk Barney to his. Come on, Barney."

As they walked, Barney asked, "Who's this fella, Charley?"

"This is a friend of Dodge's, Clint Adams."

Barney stopped and turned, gaping at Clint.

"You brung a gunman to kill me?" he asked. "The Gunsmith?"

"He's the Gunsmith, but he ain't here ta kill ya, ya blamed fool," Charley said. "We're takin' ya back to stand trial."

"For killin' that skunk?" Barney demanded. "You know what he was doin' with my wife?"

"Everybody knows, Barney."

"What?" Riggs asked. "Then I'm a laughingstock? And you're gonna take me back?"

"You shoulda thought of that before ya killed him," Charley said.

"Are they gonna hang me?" he demanded.

"Probably," Clint said.

"What?"

Clint shrugged.

"You probably would've had a better chance for mercy if you had killed your wife, Riggs," Clint said.

THIRTY

Outside of Tombstone, Charley Smith called their progress to a halt.

"Mrs. Riggs, you can go on home and tell Ol' Bannock what's goin' on."

"I want to ride in—"

"You go on and git, now," Charley told her. "No tellin' what'll happen when we ride in with Barney. Hudson had some friends in town."

"Go on, Linda," Riggs said. "Tell Pa. He'll know what to do."

She hesitated, then said, "All right."

As she rode off, Dodge asked Barney, "What do you think Bannock's gonna do, Barney?"

"I don't know," Barney said, "but Pa usually knows what to do."

Bob Hatch was very happy when they rode into Tombstone with Barney Riggs. No matter who caught the man,

Hatch's office would take the credit for bringing Barney Riggs in for murder.

A few people followed their progress on foot to the jailhouse, but no one made a move on them as they walked Riggs into the jail.

One man took one look at them, turned and ran.

"Who was that?" Clint asked.

"One of the Hudson hands," Dodge said. "I'm sure he's ridin' back to the ranch to tell 'em we got Barney."

"What will they do?"

Dodge shrugged.

"Charley, you sonofabitch," Hatch said, after Charley returned from the cell block. "How'd you know where he'd be?"

"I just played a hunch, Sheriff."

"And you had to sneak out of town to do it?" Hatch asked. "You couldn't take me along?"

"You play a hunch alone, Sheriff," Charley said. "You know that."

"You took Dodge and Adams along," Hatch said, looking at the other two men, who were both sitting across from him.

"Well, sometimes ya need a friend or two along to back yer hunch."

Charley was making it very clear that he didn't consider Hatch a friend.

"Well," Hatch said, "I guess it doesn't matter. We got him."

"Yes, sir," Charley Smith said, "we got 'im."

* * *

Dodge took Clint and Charley to his house for some whiskey.

"I wanna go and change my clothes," he said.

Charley didn't care to change, and Clint figured he'd do it later, at his hotel. Dodge seemed to want some company at his house.

He had a small place at the north end of town, just a shack, really. Clint noticed, as they entered, it was real clean.

Dodge got the bottle and three glasses and they sat at what looked like a home-made kitchen table, big enough for four people.

He poured three glasses, and they drank.

"What's botherin' ya, Fred?" Charley asked.

"I don't think this is gonna end with Barney's arrest," he said.

"'Course it ain't," Charley said. "We got to get him to trial."

"Hudson hands should be ridin' in soon," Dodge said. "And ol' man Bannock may ride in with some of his outfit."

"Think we got us a war brewin'?" Charley asked.

"Trouble, yeah," Dodge said. "A war? Maybe."

"What about Hatch?" Clint asked. "Does he realize what could happen?"

"I don't know about Hatch," Dodge said. "He sure didn't seem to be in a hurry to bring Barney in."

"Maybe he was thinking about just this," Clint said. "A possible clash of the outfits."

"Well, he's got it now," Dodge said. "Mark Smith is our district attorney. He better work on gettin' this trial put together quick."

Clint finished his whiskey and rejected the offer of a second.

"I'm going back to my hotel to change my clothes, too," he said. "See you later at the Bird Cage?"

"I'll be there," Dodge said.

Clint left, with Charley Smith in tow.

THIRTY-ONE

Wearing clean clothes and fresh from a pitcher-and-bowl bath, Clint was standing at the bar in the Bird Cage, drinking beer and eating free hardboiled eggs. He knew the eggs were salted, to make you drink more beer, but he didn't care.

He had just bitten one in half when Dodge entered and joined him at the bar.

"Those are salted, ya know," Dodge said.

"I don't care," Clint said.

"Yeah, me neither." Dodge signaled the bartender for a cold beer.

"Where's Charley?" Clint asked.

"I think he turned in early," Dodge said. "Charley's not so young, anymore."

Clint laughed. "None of us are."

"Speak for yourself," Dodge said. "I still got plenty of time ahead of me. Plenty to do."

"You've been doing this a long time," Clint said.

"I know it."

"Do you still find it gratifying?"

Dodge hesitated, then said, "It's important."

"Not exactly the same thing."

"I know."

Angel came walking over and linked her arm in Clint's.

"Hello, Deputy."

"Miss Angel. You look lovely tonight."

"Why, thank you, sir."

"And hello to you," she said, squeezing up tight next to Clint.

"Angel."

"We heard that you brought in Barney Riggs."

"Charley Smith brought him in," Dodge said. "We backed him up."

"So there's gonna be a trial?" she asked.

"Definitely."

"Why?" Clint asked. "What's your interest?"

"Not me," she said, "but a lot of the Hudson outfit visit the girls downstairs, and they've been saying there's going to be trouble if Barney Riggs is brought back to town."

"Where'd they expect us to bring him?"

"From what I heard, they wanted you to leave him in the ground out there, somewhere."

"Well, that wasn't gonna happen," Dodge said. "Miss Angel, if you'll excuse me, I got to make my rounds."

"Of course, Deputy," she said. "Have a good night."

Dodge nodded at Clint and left.

"Angel, are there any of the Hudson outfit downstairs now?"

"I don't think so," she said. "When they got word that Barney had been brought in they left."

"Probably went back to the ranch to stir up trouble," Clint said.

"What do you care?" she asked. "You don't wear a badge. You just have to worry about me stirring up trouble for you, mister."

He laughed and said. "Oh, you're trouble, all right, but Dodge is a friend of mine. And I was one of the men who brought Riggs in. If there's trouble because of it, I can't walk away now."

"Well," she said, "just don't get yourself hurt." She put her hand on his chest. "I want you at full strength."

"Don't you have work to do?" he asked, smiling to take the sting out of the question.

"Yeah, I do," she said, "but I'll see you later, Mr. Gunsmith."

He watched her walk away, then finished his beer and left the Bird Cage.

From the back of the Bird Cage, where he could see Clint and Dodge but they could not see him, John Shaunessy watched them interact with Angel, then watched Dodge walk out of the place. Finally, he stood up so he could watch Clint leave.

"What's goin' on, John?" one of the men at his table asked.

"That's what I'd like to know," the miner said. "Remember the last time Adams was in town?"

"No," the other man said.

"We did our duty and hung John Heath," Shaunessy said. "Remember that?"

"Oh, yeah, I remember."

"And both Dodge and Adams had some harsh things to say about that."

"So what?" the other man asked. "Heath got hung, he's gone, it's over."

"Naw," Shaunessy said, "it ain't over. When somebody talks like that to me, it ain't hardly over."

"So whataya gonna do?"

"I don't know," Shaunessy said, "but I'll think of something."

THIRTY-TWO

Clint walked over to the sheriff's office and entered. It was quiet, but he knew somebody had to be there because they had a prisoner. He was about to go and have a look in the cell block when Bob Hatch came walking out from there. He stopped, startled for the moment, then relaxed when he saw it was Clint.

"Adams, hey."

"Bob. What's going on?"

"Hmm? Oh, nothin'. I was just talkin', uh, to young Barney."

"About what?"

Hatch thought a moment, then shrugged and said, "I was askin' what he wanted to eat. That's part of my job, ya know?"

"Mmm, yeah," Clint said.

Hatch walked around his desk and sat down, making himself comfortable before speaking again.

"So, what brings you here?"

"I heard some talk at the Bird Cage about the boys from the Hudson outfit."

"Comin' in and causin' trouble, right?" Hatch asked. "Yeah, I heard."

"What are you going to do?"

"My job, Adams," Hatch said. "That's what I always do."

"You got enough deputies?"

"Deputies, constables," Hatch said, waving a hand. "I think we can handle a few drunken cowboys. Why, you want a badge?"

"No, no," Clint said, "that's okay. I just wanted to warn you."

"I appreciate it. Anything else?"

"Nope," Clint said. "Nothing else. Good night, Sheriff."

"'Night, Adams."

He turned and left the office. He couldn't help but wonder about Dodge's comments concerning Hatch maybe not wanting to bring Riggs in. What else could he have been talking about with Riggs.

He decided to go and find Dodge, who was probably still making his rounds.

Clint found Dodge checking doors on the corner of Sixth and Allen streets. Dodge turned and jumped back until he realized it was Clint.

"Crap, Clint," Dodge complained, "you scared the hell out of me."

"Sorry."

"Why aren't you at the Bird Cage?" Dodge asked. Then he leered and added, "Or in your hotel room with the willing Angel?"

"I wanted to talk to Hatch about the Hudson boys," Clint said. "Angel told me some more about what they've been saying to the crib girls and I figure they're on their way here to cause some trouble."

"You think they'll try to break Riggs out to lynch him?"

"Could be."

Dodge frowned.

"We had enough of that three years ago, with John Heath."

"I remember," Clint said. He didn't mention that he'd gone over that whole incident again in his head while taking a bath. "Whatever happened to that fellow, John Shaunessy?"

"Nothin'," Dodge said, "absolutely nothin'. He still works in the mines."

"Haven't seen him around, have you?"

"Not tonight. What did Hatch say?"

"Not much, just that he knew about it and would do his job, but something odd happened."

"What?"

"When I walked into the office he was in the cell block, with Riggs."

"Why?"

"He said he was talking to him. When I asked what about he came up with a story of asking him what he wanted for breakfast."

"And you don't believe him?"

"Do you? You're the one who said he didn't really want to bring Riggs in."

"I said maybe he wouldn't bring him in."

"You said he didn't want to, or wouldn't bring him in."

"Okay, so I said that."

"What if Riggs isn't in his cell, anymore?"

Dodge stared at Clint for a long moment, then said, "Let's go and find out."

THIRTY-THREE

When they entered the jail, Bob Hatch was at his desk. He looked up at them in surprise.

"Dodge, thought you were doin' your rounds," Hatch said. "Back again, Adams?"

"I ran into Dodge outside," he said.

"I told Clint I wanted to relieve you, let you go and get a drink," Dodge said. "He offered to keep me company."

"A break does sound good," Hatch said. "Maybe one beer and a change of clothes." As Hatch spoke he seemed to be a bit puzzled by the offer.

"Take your time," Dodge said. "Charley ought to be in here soon."

"I thought he turned in."

"Charley only sleeps a few hours a day," Dodge said. "He'll be around."

"Well . . . okay," Hatch said. He grabbed his hat and stood up. "But I won't be long."

"Whenever," Dodge said. "Don't worry about it."

Hatch nodded and headed for the door, but still didn't seem fully committed.

When the door closed, Dodge said to Clint, "Let's go have a look."

They both headed for the cell block. Only one cell was occupied, and it was all the way at the end. They couldn't see Riggs until they actually reached the cell. He was lying on the cot against the back wall. He was awake with his left arm across his forehead. When he heard them he dropped his arm and turned his head.

"Come to gloat?" he asked.

"Just checkin', Barney," Dodge said.

"Where'd you think I'd be?"

"Actually," Clint said, "we were just checking to make sure you're still alive."

"Why wouldn't I be?" Riggs asked. "I ain't about to hang myself, you know."

"You might not have to," Dodge said.

"Whataya mean by that?"

"We heard the Hudson outfit may be coming in to do that for you," Clint said.

Riggs sat up, slapping his feet down onto the floor.

"What?"

"Just a rumor," Dodge said.

"You can't let 'em take me," Riggs said. "You got to protect me."

"Hey," Dodge said. "I'll do my job, but that's about all I can do."

"Where's Bob?" Riggs demanded. "Where's Sheriff Hatch?"

"He went home to freshen up," Dodge said. "He should be back later."

"Does he know about this?"

"He's the sheriff," Dodge said, "he better know."

Riggs got up, rushed to the front of the cell, and grabbed the bars. He pressed his face between two of them.

"Get me out of here, Dodge," Riggs said. "Put me someplace else."

"Hey," Dodge said. "You're in a cell, where you belong."

"But—"

"If I was you," Clint said, "I'd move that cot away from that window. Don't want to make it too easy for somebody who wants to kill you."

Clint and Dodge started walking out of the cell block, with Riggs continuing to shout after them to get him out of there.

"So, he's still there," Clint said.

"I didn't think Hatch would let him out, not just like that."

"Maybe he's planning to let him escape."

"Maybe," Dodge said. "But not while I'm here—or Charley."

"Was that true about Charley?"

"Oh yeah, he don't sleep much," Dodge said. "When he says he's turnin' in, you can pretty much depend on the fact that you'll see him three hours later."

Bob Hatch walked into the Bird Cage, approached the bar, and asked for a beer. He looked around, didn't see anything of interest to him. The place was real busy, and all he could see was a crush of bodies. Briefly he considered going down to the cribs, but that wasn't really something he had to do. He had a wife at home, and he had the woman next door, who he was having an affair with. He was very friendly with his neighbor. In fact, the man had helped him out of financial troubles more than once, but that didn't stop Hatch from sleeping with the man's wife, who was very susceptible to flattery.

If he could get a message to her . . . but no. It was too short notice. Maybe after this beer he'd go home for a change of clothes, and have sex with his wife before going back to work. He'd have to wake her up, or else he could just poke her while she slept. She wasn't all that interested in sex anymore, and sometimes she hardly moved at all. That was one reason why he looked to the woman next door. Cheating sure added a lot more energy to things.

He was finishing up his beer and getting ready to leave when he noticed a man walking toward him.

"Hello, John," Hatch said.

"Bob," John Shaunessy said. "Talk to you about somethin'?"

THIRTY-FOUR

Dodge had put a pot of coffee on, and he and Clint were sitting around with their feet on the sheriff's desk, drinking it when Charley Smith walked in. He walked right to the coffeepot and poured himself some.

"Where's Bob?"

"I told him to get a drink and some rest," Dodge said. "He'll be back."

"Everything okay?" Charley asked.

"Depends on what you mean by okay," Dodge said.

Charley stared at Dodge.

"And what do you mean by okay, Fred?"

Dodge told Charley about the rumblings Clint had heard about the Hudson boys, and about Hatch's talking to Barney Riggs while nobody was around.

"I'd expect trouble from them Hudson boys," Charley said, "and from ol' man Bannock and his hands."

"You know them all better than I do," Dodge said.

"When would they be comin' in, do ya think? Before or after the trial?"

"I don't think those boys are gonna care if Barney gets convicted or not. As far as they're concerned, he did it. He killed their boss."

"That's what I figured," Dodge said.

"So what do we do?" Clint asked. "Just stand guard?"

"That's the job," Dodge said. "Our job. Me and Charley."

"Any other deputies?"

"A couple," Dodge said, "and we can call in the constables." He looked at Charley. "It's gonna be our job to guard the members of the jury. Take them to and from the hotel during the trial. Make sure they don't talk to anyone."

"Sounds like you're going to be stretched pretty thin," Clint said. "What about some of men you use for posse members? Would they help?"

"They'll probably take sides," Dodge said. "The Riggs outfit, and the Hudson outfit. Or they won't wanna get in the middle."

"Sounds like you're going to need me."

Dodge grinned.

"That's what I was hoping you'd say."

"What do you want me to do?"

"Don't know yet," Dodge said, "but it'll be good to have you around."

"I'll be here," Clint said, standing up.

"Where are you going?" Dodge asked.

"Back to my hotel," Clint said. "I didn't mean I'd actually be *here*, all the time."

"I get it. See you in the morning."

"'Night, Charley."

"See ya, Adams."

Clint left the office, headed for the hotel.

"Whataya think?" Charley asked.

"I think we're gonna have a mess on our hands tryin' to get Riggs tried. I'll talk to Mark Smith in the morning."

"And what about Bob?"

"Hatch is the boss," Dodge said, "but we better keep an eye on him."

"Agreed."

"I'm gonna go turn in, myself," Dodge said, getting up. "Hatch'll be back soon."

"I'll be here," Charley said.

"I'll talk to some of the boys in the mornin'," Dodge said, "see how many extra we can count on."

"I don't think anybody not wearin' a badge is gonna want to deal themselves in on this," Charley said.

"Yeah, well . . ." Dodge said, and left.

THIRTY-FIVE

Within a few days Riggs was indicted for murder with trial set for the following week, the Honorable Judge Webster Street presiding. Jury selection was set for Monday.

Barney Riggs continued to occupy his cell, having pushed his cot over into one corner. He was usually sitting on it, or curled up into a ball to make a small target of himself.

Dodge, Hatch, and Charley Smith took turns sitting in the office, seeing to Riggs's needs. They fed him, and kept him alive—although keeping him alive didn't seem to be much of a problem. For some reason the Hudson boys had not made a move to break him out and hang him, and ol' man Bannock and his hands had made no move to rescue him. This confused Dodge and Charley Smith, who had read those men totally different.

The day before the jury selection Dodge, Charley Smith, and Clint sat in the office and discussed it. Hatch was out doing his rounds.

* * *

"I don't get it," Charley Smith said. "My read on those Hudson boys was that they'd try to break him out and string him up."

"Maybe they still will," Clint said.

"What's takin' them so long?" Charley asked.

"Maybe there's a cool head out there," Dodge said, "convincing them to let the law handle it for them."

"What if they don't find him guilty?" Charley asked.

"They will."

"What if they don't hang him?"

"Then we'll probably have some trouble," Dodge admitted.

"What about Bannock?" Clint asked. "What's the old man waiting for? I thought he'd try to save his son, by now."

"Especially since everybody knows we don't have any help," Charley said. "Nobody in town wants to end up in the middle of a war."

They had even had two deputies quit on them.

Dodge looked at Clint.

"Maybe they know we have Clint," he suggested. "Maybe they don't want to face the Gunsmith."

"The Hudson boys, maybe," Clint said. "But I don't think that'd stop a father from trying to save his son."

"Maybe he don't wanna save his son," Dodge said.

"Why not?" Charley asked.

"The woman?" Clint said. "His son's wife?"

Dodge shrugged.

"If they were sharin' her," he said, "maybe now he

figures he don't have to. Barney's in jail, and Hudson's dead. The old man's got the woman all to hisself."

Charley carried the coffeepot around and filled their cups for them, then replaced it. He sat back down with his own cup and shook his head.

"I don't know about you boys, but that makes me feel kinda sick to my stomach."

"I know what you mean," Clint said.

Bob Hatch came in then, crossed to the coffee put, got about a half a cup out of it.

"You an unofficial deputy now, Adams?" he asked, accusingly.

"I just come in for the coffee, Bob," Clint said, raising his cup.

Hatch frowned.

"What's the word around town, Bob?" Dodge asked.

"Gonna be lots of folks at the jury selection tomorrow," Hatch said, "and at the trial. We're gonna have to collect guns at the door."

"Why?" Dodge asked. "You know somebody's gonna smuggle in a gun or two."

"Somebody's bound to try somethin', Fred," Hatch said. "The old man or the Hudson hands. Don't know what they've been waitin' for, but they gotta figure it'll be easier to break him out of court than out of jail."

"We was just talkin' about that, Bob," Charley Smith said.

"Well, I don't see how we can allow a courtroom full of guns," Hatch said.

"Okay, Bob," Dodge said. "We'll collect guns."

"Okay," Hatch said, putting his cup down. "I'll tell the mayor."

"The mayor?" Dodge asked.

"And the district attorney," Hatch said. "That's what they wanted."

He headed for the door.

"And Charley?" he said.

"Yeah?"

"Make a fresh pot of coffee, and try to leave some for the boss, huh?"

"Sure, boss," Charley said.

THIRTY-SIX

Linda Riggs didn't understand it. The old man seemed to have more stamina than Barney or Hudson ever did. He had her on all fours now, and was taking her from behind, rutting and snorting like a bull. It seemed to go on forever, and then finally he bellowed and emptied his seed into her. He flopped down on the bed next to her, trying to catch his breath. Her plan to fuck him into a heart attack didn't seem to be working, although he was pretty red in the face.

She turned over, cleaned herself with the edge of the sheet, then stood up, holding a shirt between her legs.

"When are we gonna rescue Barney, Pa?" she asked.

"I told you," he said, breathlessly, "we gotta wait for the right time."

"What about the Hudson hands?" she asked. "Sooner or later they're gonna try to kill 'im."

"Not until after the trial."

"How do you know that?"

"I've been talkin' to somebody."

"Who?"

He opened his eyes and looked at her.

"Don't you worry, girl. You just go and see about supper. You sure help a man build up an appetite."

She decided to cook him a feast. Maybe she could get him to choke to death.

The hands were just sitting around in the barn at the Hudson spread. Their boss had lived alone, and now that he was dead they had no idea what was going to happen to their jobs.

"He got any relatives, maybe back East?" one of them asked.

"Don't know."

They all looked at Sam Turner.

"Sam, you're the foreman," somebody said.

"That's right, foreman," Sam said. "That didn't mean me and the boss was friends, because we wasn't. So I don't have no idea who owns the ranch now, and I don't know what's gonna happen to our jobs."

"Maybe I can help?"

They all looked up at the man who had just entered the barn.

"What's on your mind, Shaunessy?" Sam Turner asked.

The foreman of the Grand Central Mine shrugged and said, "Just thought I might be able to help."

THIRTY-SEVEN

The next morning jury selections began. The public was allowed to attend, for the jury would be culled from their numbers.

At the door Fred Dodge and Bob Hatch collected guns from people who entered. A board had been erected with nails hammered into it, and each gun belt or gun was hung on a nail that had a number beneath it. The gun's owner was given a slip of paper with a corresponding number. They could collect their weapon on the way out.

Dodge and Hatch were wearing their guns, so they'd be able to enforce the rule.

Clint sat in a corner of the courtroom. Dodge convinced Hatch to let him keep his gun, in case they needed his help.

When asked for his gun one man pointed at Clint and asked, "Why does he get to keep his? He ain't wearin' no badge."

"That's Clint Adams, the Gunsmith," Fred Dodge said. "You wanna go and ask him for his gun?"

The man scowled, handed over his gun and sat down.

Once the courtroom was full Dodge took up a position in front of all the guns, stood with his hands clasped in front of him.

D.A. Mark A. Smith got to his feet when the bailiff shouted, "All rise. Court is in session, the Honorable Judge Webster Street presiding."

Judge Street, his thirtieth year on the bench, entered and sat in his chair behind the bench. He looked around, banged his gavel unnecessarily. It was a habit with him. Ever since his first day on the bench, he loved banging his gavel.

Clint watched with interest as the lawyers began interviewing potential jurors. Somehow, Bannock Riggs had gotten a very experienced lawyer to represent Barney. Dodge told him that the Riggs family had been in court so often they knew the system, and ol' Bannock knew how to use it.

They interviewed men young and old, mostly ones who lived in or around town. Halfway through the day they had eight of their twelve. The proceedings looked to be boring Judge Webster Street, who several times seemed to be dozing.

When they broke for lunch, Dodge and Hatch had to return guns to men, then collect them again after lunch. However, it wasn't as time consuming after because many of the attendees from the morning session did not return.

Jury selection went into a second day, pretty much a repeat of the first, but the lawyers were working quickly and efficiently and by the end of day two they had their twelve jurors, and two alternates.

Fred Dodge was named as Guard for the Person of the Court. This meant he had to be with the jury wherever they went. He'd have to take them to lunch, make sure they didn't talk to anyone, and then take them to the hotel after the days in court, once again making sure they discussed the case with no one.

But that wouldn't happen until the trial started, and that wasn't scheduled until the following week.

After the jury was selected Clint found himself in the Crystal Palace having a beer with Fred Dodge and Charley Smith. Hatch was in his office, keeping an eye on Barney Riggs.

"Are we more trusting of Hatch, all of a sudden?" Clint asked, looking at the other two men.

"With the jury picked and the trial date set I don't think Bob is gonna do anythin' that would bring attention to him," Dodge said. "I mean, if he had any intentions of doin' . . . somethin'."

Clint shrugged, sipped his beer.

"Clint, I'd like to ask you to help Charley collect the guns when the trial starts," Dodge said, then.

"Sure, but don't you have to clear that with Sheriff Hatch?" Clint asked.

"Don't worry," Dodge said. "He'll go along with it."

"I got rounds," Charley said, putting his empty mug down. "See you boys, later."

"If I don't see you, Charley," Clint said, "I'll meet you in front of the courthouse in the morning."

"Gotcha."

Charley left.

"I don't get it, Fred," Clint said. "Why don't you just run for sheriff next election?"

"You know why, Clint," Dodge said. "I wouldn't be able to give the job the time it deserves."

"You'd do a better job than Hatch is doing, wouldn't you?"

"Well, yeah . . . but I could be called away at any time."

"Have good deputies," Clint said. "Men you could trust while you're away."

"You?"

"No, not me," Clint said, "but Charley's a good man."

"Yeah, he is."

"I'm sure there are a few others."

"If Ike Roberts and Bill Daniels were here they'd be useful."

"Are they coming back?"

"Maybe, but not in time for this."

"Well, give it some thought," Clint said. "Cochise County would benefit from having you as its sheriff."

"There's no guarantee I'd even win an election," Dodge said.

"I think you'd win."

Dodge rubbed his face with both hands.

"You want another beer?" Clint asked.

"Sure."

He got up to walk to the bar, stopped when he saw five men standing just inside the batwing doors. They were all armed, and looking at him—or Dodge—or both.

"Fred."

"Yeah?"

"Isn't this gentleman's name Shaunessy?"

Dodge looked up, frowned, and stood next to Clint.

"Yeah, that's him."

"I remember," Clint said. "Grand Central Mine, right?"

"That's right."

"Those Grand Central men with him?"

"Nope," Dodge said, "those are Hudson outfit boys."

"Well," Clint said, "I guess it's about time."

"Five against two," Dodge said. "Whataya think of those odds?"

"I think we've got them right where we want them."

THIRTY-EIGHT

"You want somethin', Shaunessy?" Dodge asked.

It grew quiet in the saloon.

"Yeah, I been wantin' somethin' for three years, Dodge," the miner said, "ever since you bad-mouthed me over hanging John Heath."

"You deserved bad-mouthing, Shaunessy," Clint said. "You broke the law and murdered a man."

"I hung a murderer," Shaunessy said. "That ain't breakin' the law."

"It sure is," Dodge said. "What about you boys? Why are you standin' with this man over a three-year-old beef? I got no argument with you."

"We want Barney Riggs," one man said. "He's in your jail."

"What's one got to do with the other?" Dodge asked. "Did this man talk you into backin' his play? Where's your foreman? Where's Sam Turner?"

"Turner wouldn't stand with us," another man said. "He's turned yella."

"Sam Turner's no coward," Dodge said. "He just picks his battles, and this ain't his. It ain't yours, neither. Shaunessy, tell these men to go home."

"I ain't leavin' without your hide, Dodge."

"Fine," Dodge said. "Face me man-to-man. Why involve them?"

"Sure, you got Adams backin' your play, I'm supposed to stand alone?"

"Adams won't take a hand," Dodge promised. "Just you and me."

Shaunessy licked his lips. Clint could see the hesitation in his eyes, but the men standing behind him couldn't see it.

"I won't make a move, Shaunessy," Clint promised.

"I ain't no gunman."

"No guns," Dodge said. "Just you and me."

"Go on, Shaunessy," one of the Hudson men said, "take 'im. Then we'll go and break Riggs out and hang him."

"Nobody's hangin' anybody," Clint said. "There's a trial going on. Leave it to the law, boys."

"That was our boss Riggs killed," another said.

"You better talk it over with your foreman, then," Clint said. "This man doesn't care about you or your dead boss. He's got his own axe to grind, and he's trying to get you to do it for him."

"Come on, John," Dodge said. "Drop your gun belt and face me."

"Yeah, come on, Shaunessy," one of the hands shouted. "Show 'im."

"You boys, you draw and take 'em," Shaunessy said. "Take 'em both."

The four men hesitated, then one said, "Well, if'n you ain't a gunman, Shaunessy, we sure as hell ain't."

"And that there's the Gunsmith," another said.

"See, boys?" Clint asked. "Who's yella now?"

"Drop your gun belt, John, or turn and walk out," Dodge said. "Them's your choices."

Shaunessy licked his lips again, his eyes flicked back and forth between Dodge and Clint, his hands closed into fists.

"Damn you!" he snapped, then turned and pushed through the four men who were backing him.

"You boys want to push this any further?" Clint asked the remaining men.

Now it was their turn to lick their lips, and then they turned together and walked out.

"Been waitin' three years for Shaunessy to make his move," Dodge said, as he and Clint sat back down and business in the saloon resumed.

"Kind of disappointing, wasn't it?" Clint asked.

THIRTY-NINE

The first day of the trial the room was packed. Clint and Charley Smith collected all the guns, but they were too heavy to hang on the wall, so they just had to pile them in a corner. When it came time for men to get their guns back they could just look for themselves.

The Case of the Territory of Arizona vs. Barney Riggs got under way.

Clint wasn't very interested in what both sides had to say. His only interest was in the outcome. Men arguing in court had never held much fascination for him. Particularly when they argued for hours and hours and nothing seemed to get done.

He could barely stay awake as the arguments went on for two days. On the third day he decided to walk the jury over to the Can Can restaurant with Dodge, where they had set up a table for sixteen—the jurors, Dodge, and room for one more lawman—or whoever.

Today the "whoever" was Clint Adams.

*   *   *

Dodge and Clint walked the jury to the Can Can in a straight line. At one point, as the center of the line of jurors was passing the entrance to the O.K. Corral—owned by a man named John Montgomery—shots rang out.

The jurors scattered looking for cover. Clint and Dodge drew their guns and sought out the shooters. They saw them standing just inside the corral.

Dodge was at the head of the jury, Clint at the back end. They each collected their men and got them under cover, then joined one another across the street from the corral.

"Ironic, isn't it?" Dodge asked.

"Yeah."

Clint recognized Bannock Riggs. There was another man with him he did not know.

"See 'em?" Dodge asked.

"Yeah, Bannock and another man."

"I don't know the other one," Dodge said. "Listen, Bannock's no gunman, but the other one—"

"I'll take him, you take the old man. He was probably shooting at you, anyway."

"Right."

"Talk to him."

Dodge nodded, then shouted, "Bannock. This ain't the way, old man."

No answer.

"Come on, Bannock. You're not gonna get Barney off this way."

"I ain't lookin' to get him off," Bannock answered, "just away."

"Well, that ain't gonna happen, either," Dodge said, "so you and your friend might as well come out and drop your guns."

"I want my boy, Dodge," Bannock said. "You're gonna have to kill me or give 'im to me."

"You're makin' a big mistake, old man."

"You're probably right," Bannock said, surprising both Dodge and Clint with the admission, "but I can't figure out no other way."

"Let nature take its course," Dodge suggested. "Let the trial go on."

"They'll hang 'im!"

"You don't know that for sure. If you give up, though, you'll be alive to see what happens. If you die here, then he might hang, anyway."

They were greeted with silence. Clint could still see the two men inside the corral.

"I've got a shot," he told Dodge.

"Wait," Dodge said. "I may still be able to talk him out."

"Yeah, but what about the other one?"

"He'll go along with Bannock," Dodge said, holstering his gun. "Give me a chance."

"If either one of them even looks at you funny, I'm firing."

Dodge made a wait gesture with his hands and stood up. He put his hands in the air. "Keep the jurors under cover."

He stepped out into the open.

"Bannock, I just wanna talk."

Clint heard the sound of a hammer cocking. He didn't

know if it was Bannock Riggs's gun or the other one, but he could see enough of each man to have a shot.

"Take it easy," Dodge said. "This ain't the way. Your boy wouldn't want this."

Bannock laughed.

"My boy wouldn't care one way or the other, Dodge," he said. "To tell you the truth, I don't much care, neither, but he's my boy. I'm supposed to do somethin'."

"Sure you are, Bannock, but not get yourself killed," Dodge said. "Holster your guns. Clint Adams has got you both in his sights."

Both men moved, then, but Clint felt he still had a shot.

"Come on, Bannock," Dodge said. "I've got some hungry jurors here. What's it gonna be?"

"Goddamn, old man!" the other man said. He stepped out and took aim at Dodge, impatient with Bannock. Clint shot him down with one bullet to the heart. He fell into the dirt, wafting a cloud of dust right next to Bannock Riggs.

The old man tossed his gun out into the street.

With Bannock arrested and placed in a cell, Dodge came back to the Can Can, where Clint was sitting with the jurors.

"You took a hell of a chance, Fred," Clint said, as the man sat down next to him.

"Not really," Dodge said. "I knew two things."

"What two things?"

"I knew Bannock wouldn't shoot me," Dodge said. "The old man's not a killer."

"And the second thing?"

Dodge grinned.

"I knew you wouldn't let me get killed out there like a fool, with my hands up."

FORTY

Bannock did have a plan.

It had been his intention to send the jury scattering, thereby causing a mistrial. Then he was going to have his lawyer file for a change of venue. Now it was up to the judge to decide if the jury had been tampered with. They had been instructed not to talk to anyone— including one another—about the case. They had not discussed the case, but everyone knew that after being shot at, they were thinking about it.

The judge had to decide if this was reason enough to disband the jury and declare a mistrial.

Clint and Dodge were questioned, assured the judge that they had kept the jury members together during the shooting. Then the jurors were questioned. It took a whole day away from the actual trial, but in the end Judge Webster Street decided to keep the jury together and continue the next morning with the trial.

Dodge went to the jail to tell Bannock that his plan

had not worked. Hatch had put Bannock in a cell right next to his son, who was sitting on his cot morosely.

After Dodge delivered the news and left, Barney said to Bannock, "You're a useless old man."

"You're no-account and you always was," Bannock said.

"You think Linda's gonna stay with you after they hang me, don't ya? Well, she ain't."

"A lot you know," the old man said. "She's happier now than she's ever been. She don't have to worry about you no more, or Hudson. Just me."

"You disgust her."

The old man laughed.

"She's happy to have a man between her legs who's full growed."

"You sonofabitch."

"Bastard."

They fell silent, and after a few moments Barney said, "They're gonna kill me, Pa."

"Your lawyer might still get ya off," Bannock said.

"What if he don't?"

"They ain't gonna keep me in here forever, son," Bannock said. "We'll figure somethin' out."

"You gotta get me out, Pa," Barney said. "And don't try to do it yerself. Hire somebody. Get a gunny in here to handle that Gunsmith, and get me out of here."

"Like I said, son," Bannock replied, "we'll figure somethin' out."

FORTY-ONE

The trial recommenced the next morning, and this time there weren't so many guns to collect. Seemed folks were worried now that there might be a shooting in the courtroom itself.

Fred Dodge's seat in the court was right up alongside District Attorney Mark A. Smith's table. Charley Smith sat in the back—or Bob Hatch, whichever was there. Clint sat by the collected guns, to be sure no one grabbed one from the wall.

The trial went on for three days, until finally the attorneys had to make their closing arguments. The defense went first, and Clint didn't hear anything in the man's address that he thought would sway the jury.

The district attorney went next. Dodge, in the chair next to the desk, had his short double-barreled shotgun across his thighs, and seemed to be on the lookout for trouble. If there was going to be an outburst in the courtroom, it would be about that time, while the D.A. was making his closing remarks.

Smith began to describe what he imagined happened that night. How Barney Riggs had sneaked over to the Hudson ranch, waited in the dark for Hudson to appear, and then crept up on him from behind . . .

". . . and he did then murder Hudson!" he finished, with great dramatic flair.

There was a large ink stand on each attorney's table, and Barney Riggs leaped to his feet and grabbed it up.

"Yes, you sonofabitch, and I'm gonna kill you, too!" he shouted at Smith.

Clint watched as Dodge moved incredibly fast. He sprang from his seat onto Barney's shoulders, crashing to the floor with him. Dodge grabbed the ink stand from Barney's hand, then dragged him to his feet and tossed him back into his chair. Dodge then reversed his shotgun and pointed it at the prisoner.

Mark A. Smith, as smooth as could be, turned and said to Dodge, "Thank you, Fred," and continued with his closing statement. Dodge stayed by Barney until Smith finished his argument, then the jury was led away to deliberate, and the prisoner was returned to his cell.

Court was adjourned until such time as the jury returned with their verdict. Clint and Charley Smith returned the guns to people as they left, then turned to face Dodge.

"How did you make that jump?" Charley asked.

Dodge turned and took a look, gauging the distance he had jumped.

"I don't know," he said. "I just did."

"Impressive, Fred," Clint said. "I don't think I could

have jumped that far. I probably would have shot him, ending the trial."

"It never occurred to me," Dodge said. "I just reacted."

While they were talking, Mark Smith came walking over. It was the first time Clint had seen him up close. He had the bearing of an older man, but was not yet forty.

He shook hands with Dodge and said, "Thanks again, Fred."

"You're welcome, Mark."

"Didn't think you could jump that far."

"Neither did I," Dodge said.

"Nobody could," Clint added.

They all laughed.

"So, what do you think?" Dodge asked Smith. "Guilty or not guilty."

"They'll come back with a guilty plea," Smith said, confidently. "The question is will they hang him? Takes a special kind of person to recommend a hanging."

"I guess we'll have to wait and see," Dodge said. He looked at the three men. "Anybody want to wait in a saloon?"

FORTY-TWO

The district attorney had other work to do, so he did not accompany them to the Crystal Palace for a drink. Also, Dodge couldn't go because he had to stick by the jury, even while they were deliberating. That left only Clint and Charley Smith to share a beer.

"Charley, I've been talking to Fred about running for sheriff," Clint said.

"He should," Charley said. "He'd be a good one. Better than Ward was, and better than Hatch."

"He's not sure he'd get elected."

"Oh, he'd get elected," Charley said. "'Specially if he was runnin' against Bob Hatch."

"You should talk to him about it."

"If you can't convince him, what makes you think I can?" Charley asked.

"I haven't seen him in three years, but you've been here every day," Clint pointed out. "Maybe he'll listen to you."

Charley shrugged.

"I can try. I'll tell ya, though, it sure ain't a job I'd want."

"You'd be pretty good at it," Clint said.

"Nah," Charley said. "I ain't the type to give orders. Rather take 'em—and then do what I want, anyway."

"I'll drink to that," Clint said.

In the jury room things were not going well. One man out of the twelve—a well-known man in Tombstone—had suddenly decided that he could not, in all good conscience, sentence a man to death.

"You should have said somethin' about that when they were questionin' us," another juror said.

"At that time, I thought I could do it," the man said. "I thought I could sentence a guilty man to hang, and I thought that nobody was more guilty than Barney Riggs."

"So what happened?" the jury foreman asked.

The man shrugged.

"I can't do it."

The foreman addressed the rest of the jurors.

"We can't let this be a hung jury," he said. "We have to put Riggs away while we have a chance."

"So what do we do?" another man asked. "Keep tryin' to get him to change his mind?"

"I'm not gonna change my mind," the man said.

"Fine," the foreman said. "I have a suggestion."

"What is it?"

"One that I think you can live with," the foreman said. "Let's sentence him to life."

"Life?" another man said. "He killed a man."

"Yeah," the foreman said, "but if we sentence him to life, he'll go to Yuma."

"Life in Yuma," another juror said. "That's almost as bad as hangin'."

"You said it," another man said.

"So?" the foreman asked them all.

"It's up to him," someone said, pointing to the man who'd had a sudden attack of conscience.

He nodded slowly and said, "Well, yeah, I think I can live with that."

"Okay," the foreman said. "All in favor of a life sentence for Barney Riggs. Raise your hand."

Twelve hands went up.

"Just to be sure," the foreman said, "anybody opposed?"

No hands.

"All right," he said. "We go with life."

Everybody in the courtroom was surprised when the jury foreman announced that, even though they had found Barney Riggs guilty of murder, the jury had opted for a life sentence over death.

Judge Street stared at the standing foreman for a few moments, then looked over at the D.A., who simply shrugged.

Fred Dodge thought, *Maybe I should've shot him.*

Barney Riggs was seated at the defense table with chains on his wrists, and ankles.

"Very well," Judge Street said, and the foreman sat down.

The judge thanked the members of the jury for doing their duty and dismissed them. Then he set a date for

Barney Riggs to come back into court and receive his sentence.

Once again men filed out of the courtroom and Clint returned their guns. Barney Riggs was taken back to jail by Sheriff Bob Hatch. In the front of the courtroom Mark Smith was deep in discussion with Judge Street.

Since he did not have a jury to watch over, Dodge walked over to where Clint was handing the last man his weapon.

"What do you think?" Dodge asked.

"For some reason the jury decided on leniency," Clint said. "I wouldn't have thought that."

"Me, neither. I don't get it. He clearly murdered Hudson from ambush. That's a hanging offense in any court in the country, isn't it?"

"Far as I know."

Dodge turned and looked toward the front of the room, where the judge and the D.A. were still conferring.

"The judge could still overrule," Clint said. "He could sentence Riggs to death."

"He could," Dodge said, "and Smith might be askin' him to do that right now, but I've never seen it happen before. I think he'll go along with the jury and sentence Riggs to life in Yuma."

"Where he could end up dead, anyway," Clint said, "if he's not tough enough."

"True."

"You want to get something to eat?"

"Definitely," Dodge said. "And if you don't mind, not at the Can Can."

FORTY-THREE

No one ever found out about Bob Hatch and his neighbor's wife, and in the next election he was once again chosen to represent his party on the ticket for Sheriff of Tombstone. Running against him, however, was a well-respected cattleman by the name of John Slaughter—and Slaughter won by a wide margin. Tombstone finally had itself a sheriff it could be proud of.

Fred Dodge remained in Tombstone, kept his job as deputy and as constable, and continued his undercover work for Wells Fargo. It was not until years later that he finally came out from being undercover to publicly work as a Wells Fargo agent.

Tombstone continued its decline and never again reached the height of its popularity, or fame, that it had achieved while the Earps were there.

Clint left Tombstone, learned later of Hatch's defeat at the hands of John Slaughter, but assumed that Dodge would remain there, undercover. Years later he heard something about Dodge going public as a Wells Fargo agent, and he did work again with Fred Dodge on behalf of Wells Fargo . . . but that is a story for another time.

Watch for

THE BANDIT PRINCESS

341st novel in the exciting GUNSMITH series
from Jove

Coming in May!

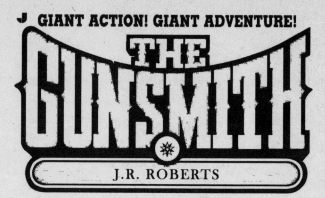

GIANT ACTION! GIANT ADVENTURE!

THE GUNSMITH

J.R. ROBERTS

penguin.com/actionwesterns

M455AS0509